The Knights of Pellagaroo

Terence Mitchell

Pen Press

First published in Great Britain by Pen Press

All paper used in the printing of this book has been made
from wood grown in managed, sustainable forests.

ISBN 978-1-78003-647-2

Printed and bound in the UK
Pen Press is an imprint of
Indepenpress Publishing Limited
25 Eastern Place
Brighton
BN2 1GJ

A catalogue record of this book is available from
the British Library

Cover design by the author

For Teresa and Francine with love from your Pa.

The Knights of Pellagaroo

To Jo and
Family with
good wishes
from
Jerry M.

Chapter 1

There had been a thunderstorm during the night. Dory had heard it rolling around the sky for several hours before it seemed to have singled out his house for special attention.

He had just managed to get off to sleep when there had been a loud bang – the roof tiles had rattled and his bedroom had lit up as bright as day. Then the storm had gone on its rambling way, the thunder had gradually quietened and, when he had looked out of the window, all that was left were a few noiseless flashes of light above the distant hills.

Quickly he wrote down a brief description of the storm's visit in an exercise book he kept on his bedside table. He had an essay to write as part of his homework and the thunderstorm would be an ideal subject.

It was a Saturday morning. The storm had blown away, the sun was shining and, best of all, it was his birthday. He had spent the last half-hour lying in bed in a pleasantly idle way, wondering what his parents had bought him for a present. He knew what he wanted it to be. He had seen it on a recent trip into town with his mother. In the centre of a shop window, making everything else there seem invisible, had stood an orange kite. This kite was *big* – as big as, and shaped like, the shield of a knight of olden days. It was a storm-riding giant with a mile of string and a long tail of coloured ribbons. He had pointed it out to his mother but, apart from 'Yes dear, very nice,' she hadn't seemed very interested.

Reluctantly, his thoughts returned to yesterday, which had not started out well. His headmaster had called out his name in assembly to congratulate him on winning first prize in a short-story competition for juniors in a national newspaper – something Dory had been trying to keep secret. Pink with embarrassment, he had tried to smile as everyone had clapped and cheered.

The smell of hot buttered toast, followed by the rattle of the teacups, came rising up the staircase and yesterday's awkward moment was soon forgotten. Down in the kitchen, his mother heard the usual 'thump' on the ceiling as he jumped out of bed.

'Happy Birthday, Dory,' she called up to him. 'Breakfast's almost ready.'

After he had quickly washed and dressed, he looked at himself in the bathroom mirror. Today he was ten years old. Somehow, he'd expected to look a bit different – a year older, a bit more grown-up. He examined his chin to see if he had grown even the smallest whisker. No, he was just the same Dory that he had been yesterday – brown-eyed, freckle-faced, mop-haired and smooth-chinned. Was it the face of a budding author? Probably not! The face suddenly grinned back at him. Who'd want to be a grown-up, he thought, as he hurried down the stairs?

In the hallway a pleasant surprise was waiting for him. Standing against the wall, too big and too awkward to wrap, was the kite from the shop window.

'Thanks, Mum! Thanks, Dad! It's the best present ever!' he shouted, as he joined them at the breakfast table.

'You be careful with that kite,' said his father. 'If a bit of a wind was to spring up, it could hoist you into the air and carry you over into the next county!'

Dory looked across to the kitchen window where the curtains were fluttering in the breeze. It was obviously going to be a great day for kite-flying. His father's words had set his imagination going and he wondered if he could use them in a story; perhaps about a young boy – or girl – who was carried away by a kite on a windy day to a strange land where...?

'Eat your breakfast before it gets cold,' said his mother, 'and stop day-dreaming!'

***

About a mile away from Dory's house was a large area of moorland. Just the place to practise his kite-flying skills. There were very few trees up there, no chimney pots to get in the way, and it was usually a bit on the breezy side. He would take some sandwiches and spend the whole day by himself. Well, it was his birthday and his mother had said that he could.

'But don't be late for your tea,' she had called after him. He smiled to himself as he waved goodbye, knowing that there would be a birthday cake and some of his friends waiting for him when he got home. Then everyone would sing 'Happy Birthday to you' as he blew out the candles.

From across the street, two small children ran over and began to follow him, and soon he heard the familiar chant that was now making the rounds.

'Dory, Dory, tell us a story!' they cried, until he suddenly turned around, screwed up his face and pretended to chase them away.

'See you later,' he called out as they ran off, laughing. 'Don't be late or all the cake will be gone!'

By the time he had climbed the hill that led to the moors, Dory was quite out of breath. Not only had the way been steep, but the force of the wind had gradually increased, making the kite difficult to hang on to. Each sudden gust made the long tail of ribbons stream out behind him with a crack and a whistle, while the big sail trembled beneath his fingers and hummed in his ears like an angry swarm of bees. It's almost as though it's alive, he thought. Alive and eager to fly.

Ahead of him was a stone wall which had been built to stop the wild ponies that lived on the moors from wandering off. There was a stile built into it, and once he had climbed over he was able to see the full extent of the land – miles and miles of purple heather which rippled in the wind like the waves on the sea until it reached the far horizon where a narrow strip of blue that really was the sea sparkled in the sunlight.

The original plan had been for him to lay the kite on the ground, unwind some of the string, give it a tug and then run with it until it rose into the air, but now the wind was so strong that the kite immediately rose up as soon as it was pulled, and with such force that it almost jerked him off his feet. Quickly, he let out more and more string until, in no time at all, the kite was soaring high into the sky with its long tail waving beneath it. Soon, he found that he had to let out more and more string to avoid being pulled over, until at last he was left hanging on to just the wooden handle at the end.

Dory remembered what his father had said about the kite carrying him into the next county and suddenly it didn't seem very funny. His arms were beginning to ache, so much so that he wondered if soon he might have to let the kite go. The thought of losing his precious birthday present on its first day out was not a happy one, but maybe, just maybe, he could run with it in the direction it wanted to go until the wind died down a little.

It didn't take him long to make up his mind. With the wind now rushing around him and the kite pulling at his outstretched arms, he began to run, sometimes leaving the ground in a series of leaps and bounds; then a hop skip and jump over some prickly bushes and a splash through a stream, scaring sheep, ponies and anything else that got in his way.

Still the wind continued to drive the kite through the sky, as though it was determined to wrench it from his grasp, and soon, with sore fingers and tiring arms, he realised that he wouldn't be able to hold on for much longer.

A few steps more and the decision was made for him. The ground fell sharply away and, as he found himself being carried through the air, he released his hold, falling several feet back to earth with a bump, rolling down the rest of the slope and ending up flat on his back with all the breath knocked out of him.

***

When he had recovered a little, he sat up and looked around. There was no sign of his kite – just a few birds circling in the distance and a small cloud hanging over his head. Rather strangely, the wind now began to die down, almost as if the kite had taken most of it away. Somewhere ahead, wind and kite must be racing through the air, or perhaps the kite had now fallen to the ground. But please, he thought, not into the branches of a tall tree!

Slowly, he got to his feet. He didn't seem to have any injuries, but his fingers were aching and his sandwiches were a bit squashed. But that was nothing compared to the loss of his kite. Ahead of him he saw that this part of the moor was gradually coming to an end, giving way to some rough grassland that sloped gently upwards and was strewn with large boulders. Here, sheep grazed among shrubs that were spiked and covered with yellow flowers, and it was in this direction that the wind had been heading when it had carried off his kite. From the top of the slope he would be able to get some idea of his bearings and, with a bit of luck, he might be able to catch sight of it.

The climb up the slope was fairly easy as it was not too steep and he was able to follow the path that the sheep had worn into the grass. They raised their heads as he weaved his way between the bushes and then, as if to say 'It's nothing to worry about, it's only a boy,' they went back to their grazing. At the top, he climbed on to one of the biggest rocks and took a good look around. The sheep path continued down the other side before disappearing into a group of trees. Beyond that, he saw a tall, dark shape, which was probably a building of some kind.

The sun was now climbing high into the sky. At home, his parents would soon be sitting down to their mid-day meal. It was toad-in-the-hole on Saturdays – his favourite. He sat down and unpacked his sandwiches. Surely he would soon find his kite and then stroll home in time for tea.

Chapter 2

The building turned out to be a big house made of grey stones. It had a tall, circular tower at one end and lots of arched windows. It looked a bit spooky. A haunted house? Perhaps this was going to turn out to be a real adventure instead of a made-up one.

Surrounding the property was a high stone wall with a pair of big iron gates at the front, but what he saw on the other side came as a pleasant surprise. The house may have looked a bit grim, but here in the gardens everything looked very nice. Green lawns took up most of the grounds, surrounded by borders filled with colourful flowers. A group of tall, graceful trees grew near the house and from one of these a child's swing was gently stirring to and fro, as if someone had just left it. But what pleased him most of all was the patch of bright orange on the grass nearby. *Could it be his kite?*

From somewhere in the trees, a bird began to sing, and then another, and soon many more joined in until the garden rang with sound. The scary feeling he had experienced on seeing the house had now left him and he decided to see if anyone was at home. The gates were tall and strong, with a pair of handles in the middle. He tried to turn them, first one way and then the other, but they would not move. He pressed his face against the bars of the gates, hoping to catch sight of someone – a gardener perhaps, or the child whose swing it was, but there was no one to be seen.

He tried the handles again, shaking them until the gates rattled, but nobody appeared. The birds stopped singing and the garden was silent again. The thought came to him that maybe he could climb over the gates, pick up the kite if it was there and make off with it – well, it *was* his kite, so it wouldn't be stealing, would it? He stepped back to look at how to do this and then saw something he hadn't noticed before – set into the wall at the side of the gates was some kind of ornament. Closer inspection showed it to be a large ear with the word 'Speak' written under it, and on the opposite side of the gates was a large mouth with the word 'Listen'.

He decided that the ear and the mouth must be a kind of telephone to ask if anyone was home. He thought a little about what he wanted to say, and then, standing on the tips of his toes, said:

'Hello, er, my name is Dory. Can I come in please and get my kite? It's my birthday present and it's landed in your garden.'

Minutes passed, perhaps as many as five, and just as he was thinking that no one was at home, a deep voice came booming out of the metal mouth.

'Enter!' it said, the word echoing around the walls of the garden. He heard the locks draw back and saw the gates swing open.

***

Leading up to the house was a winding path, which took him past small ornamental fish ponds and colourful shrubs, and now he was able to see that it was, indeed, his kite that was lying nearby.

He resisted the impulse to run over to see if it was damaged and soon he was standing at the front door of the house. On either side of it were stone sculptures of strange-looking animals. He couldn't decide if they were lions or dogs, as they looked like a cross between the two. He raised his hand to the door knocker, but before he could touch it the door swung silently open, revealing an empty hallway. He looked round to see if anyone was now in the garden and when he turned back a little girl was standing in the doorway.

'Hello,' he said, when he had recovered from his surprise. 'Please may I have my kite back?'

The girl nodded.

'Yes,' she said in a quiet voice. 'It fell from the sky this morning. It is all right for you to go and get it.'

Dory ran across to where the kite was lying. Thankfully, the kite itself was not damaged, although two of its tail ribbons were missing – a repair job for when he got home. Otherwise, he felt happy that everything seemed to be turning out so well. Back at the door, the girl was waiting for him. His head had been so full of thoughts about his kite that he had not noticed much about her appearance. Her hair was dark, parted in the middle, and it hung neatly down on either side of her head. She was small and pretty, but her eyes were red and swollen, as though she had been crying. He guessed that she was a little younger than him.

'My name is Aimi,' she said. 'I am glad you have found your kite. I hope it is not broken.'

'I'm Dory,' he replied. 'It's lost a couple of ribbons, that's all – I can easily fix it.'

'That is good,' said Aimi. 'Have you come far? Would you like some tea?'

Dory thought about the long walk home. If he left soon, he would just about be in time for his birthday celebrations.

'Well, I really should be going,' he said, but seeing how sad she looked, almost on the point of crying, he added, 'but some tea would be great, thanks.'

Aimi led the way down the hall and showed him into a well-equipped kitchen. From the window he could see more lawns and flowers. The afternoon sun glowed brightly and white doves strutted across the grass. Everything looked so peaceful, but he couldn't help feeling that something was wrong here. Where were the grown-ups? The house was full of nice furniture. The hall was hung with pictures and led to a wide staircase where there were adult hats and coats hanging from a hallstand – yet the place seemed strangely empty. Surely Aimi didn't live here all by herself?

There was a long cabinet at one side of the room and he watched as Aimi pressed one of the many buttons that ranged along it. Soon there was the hiss of steam and a bubbling brown liquid came out of a spout and into a waiting teapot. She pressed another button and a tray full of small cakes popped up.

'Please sit down,' she said, putting a chair for him at the table. When she had filled his cup and set out the cakes she sat opposite him and told him to help himself. He was now quite hungry, but he couldn't bring himself to eat anything until he had asked her why she looked so sad. But once he had begun to question her, he wished he hadn't. With her head hung down and her hands covering her face, she began to sob. It was all very sad. He wanted to say something to comfort her – anything to stop her crying – but he just couldn't think of what to do or say. In the end, he decided to keep quiet, to let her cry for a while, and then perhaps she would be able to explain what was wrong.

When Aimi had dried her eyes, she said, 'I am sorry to be a cry-baby, but I am very worried. I live here with my father, but he has disappeared. So now I am alone and I do not know what to do.'

Dory said nothing for a while. The words had shocked him so much that he wondered if he had heard her properly.

'Disappeared?' he said at last. 'Did you say he'd disappeared?'

Aimi didn't answer the question, but said, 'I must go now and try to find my brave face. Please drink your tea, and when I come back I shall tell you what I can.'

Dory ate some of the cakes and drank his tea. What Aimi had said had come as a big surprise and now he wanted to hear what else she had to say. 'Disappeared!' No, she must be mistaken! People didn't just vanish – did they?

***

When Aimi returned, she looked much better. She had washed her face and now most of the redness had gone from her eyes. She sat down and poured herself some tea.

'Yes, I am alone here,' she said, 'at least for the moment. I have not seen my father since yesterday at breakfast time. I have searched the house from top to bottom, but I cannot find him anywhere.'

Dory started to ask questions, but she held up her hand as if to stop him. He was pleased to see such a difference in her. She seemed now to be less like a little girl and more of a grown-up. The tears had gone and she was much more composed.

'My family comes from Japan,' she said. 'My mother died when I was just a baby, so I do not remember her. My father is a very clever man. He is a professor of science, an engineer, an inventor and many other things besides. His inventions have made him very rich, so now he is able to study all the things that interest him – things I do not really understand – to do with space and time, astronomy, physics, stuff like that. He has such a lot of things on his mind that I would not be surprised at anything he was involved in. Perhaps he has gone time-travelling.'

She smiled at the shocked look on Dory's face. 'I am just joking,' she added. 'He would never leave me on my own, even if he could do that. At least, not without telling me.'

Dory had questions to ask. He found some of the things she had said hard to understand. 'If your father spends so much time studying all these things, you must be alone for quite a lot of the time. And how do you manage about school – I'm sure there aren't any schools anywhere near this place?'

Aimi laughed. 'You should see my piles of homework. My father teaches me. He makes sure I learn something new every day. When he is busy, he gives me things to study, so I do not really need to go to school.'

'But don't you get lonely, in this big house, with no other children to play with?'

Aimi nodded and smiled rather sadly. 'I do sometimes, but I have my own room and plenty of toys. We have a big garden and, anyway, it is nice to be on my own so that I can read my books in peace.'

Dory was sure that Aimi was telling the truth, but how and why had her father gone off and left her? Perhaps he was one of those absent-minded professors he had read about, who put salt in their tea instead of sugar, or forgot the number of the house they lived in, or perhaps he had been called away on business and forgotten to tell her? He suddenly remembered the voice at the gates.

'But who was the man who spoke to me at the gates,' he asked, 'someone with a loud voice who told me to come in?'

Aimi began to laugh, so much so that she had to put her teacup down. 'Come with me,' she said, getting to her feet, 'and I shall introduce you to him.'

Dory followed her along the hallway, curious to know what had made her laugh. They stopped in front of a small green door.

'In here,' she said, as she stepped inside. 'Please come in.'

He hesitated, wondering who would be waiting to greet him.

'Come in,' she said again, 'there is nothing to be afraid of.' Once again she laughed and then, taking him by the hand, she led him through the doorway. Inside, Dory saw a very strange-looking room. Three of the walls were just bare brick, but the fourth was covered with a panel of switches, dials, screens and rows of twinkling lights. Looking closer, he saw that each screen appeared to show a different part of the house. Every room seemed to be included and every part of the outside of the building as well.

Aimi pointed to one of the screens which showed the garden where the doves were still wandering about. She pressed a button and he heard again the voice that had called to him earlier.

'Enter!' it said loudly, filling the room with sound. Then the gates opened, causing the doves to fly up into the trees, and after a minute or two the gates closed again and the birds returned.

'It is just a recording,' explained Aimi, 'but *this* is real.' She pressed another button and pointed to a screen that had just lit up. He saw a boy and a girl standing in front of a panel of lights and switches and, as he saw the boy raise his hand to his mouth in surprise, he laughed as he realised that he was watching Aimi and himself.

'From this room,' she continued, 'you can open the front gates, close the curtains in the living room, switch on the outside lights or water the plants in the greenhouse. The only part of the house that is not shown is my father's study.'

Dory saw a slight movement on one of the screens. Closer inspection revealed a laboratory filled with scientific instruments. Gleaming equipment stood around the walls and there were tables covered with glass containers of all shapes and sizes, some of which held coloured liquids that fizzed and bubbled. Others were filled with mysterious-looking dark substances that remained still beneath gently rising clouds of vapour.

'That is my father's laboratory,' said Aimi, 'which was the first place I looked when I was trying to find him. I also tried to open the door to his study, but it was locked.'

She pointed to a large key that was hanging on a hook close by. 'The key is here,' she added, 'so he cannot be inside – unless there are two keys.'

This is getting more and more like a detective story, thought Dory. 'Shall we take the key and have a look in there? We might find a clue of some kind – something to help find him.'

Aimi nodded. 'I have not been in there for quite a while. My father keeps it locked, but maybe now we should take a look.'

Inside the study there was not much room to move about. All around the walls were shelves full of books on astronomy, geography, maths and even magic – hundreds of books on almost every subject you could think of. There was a large desk in the middle of the room and this was covered with yet more books, piles of paper, seashells and glass cases filled with specimens of butterflies. A stuffed lizard stood in the middle of all this, beside a microscope that was surrounded by boxes and boxes of glass slides. A large brass telescope stood in front of the window, its barrel gleaming in the sunlight as it pointed at the sky.

'Well,' said Dory, after they had looked around, 'your father's not in here, that's for sure. There's not even enough room for a mouse to hide. Don't you have any idea at all where he is? Didn't he say anything about going away at breakfast time yesterday?'

Once more, Aimi was silent for a while. He had the feeling that she had something on her mind – something to do with her father that she was reluctant to talk about. He also felt that she was about to tell him what it was.

Chapter 3

'I am sure there is something strange going on in this house, but I do not know exactly what it is,' said Aimi. 'My father is a kind man, but he is also very secretive. When I ask him questions, he just tells me to wait for a while and says one day I will know everything.

'Sounds a bit odd to me,' murmured Dory. 'Whatever did he mean?

Aimi looked around the cluttered room and gave a big sigh. 'I do not know,' she said wearily. 'I only know that he is my father, and that fathers should have respect, so I stopped asking questions.'

There was an old leather settee near the window and she moved some more books and papers off it so they could sit down.

'I think that whatever has happened to him is to do with an old book he discovered when we lived in Japan. He spent a lot of time studying it and then, after a few months, we left home and came to this country and bought this house on the moor. It is a strange place. It was once used by a religious order of some sort; a retreat, I think they call it – somewhere where monks go to meditate and live a simple life. I heard my father mention once that it was built on a "ley line", but I have no idea what that is.'

Dory put up his hand. 'A prehistoric track that joins two ancient places in the landscape. We've been learning about those at school. People don't really understand what they mean, but they seem to be important in some way.'

'Well, he bought this house for a definite reason,' Aimi continued, 'and I think its position is something to do with it.'

Dory remembered the feeling he had had when he had first seen the building – a haunted house? No, he didn't feel that now, but there was something very odd about it.

'The tower,' he asked. 'What's that for? Is it something the monks used, like a bell-tower?'

Aimi shook her head. 'I have no idea what it is for, but the monks had nothing to do with it. My father had it built. He employed workmen to convert the house into the way he wanted it to be. The tower had to be built to exact measurements. He even made the men alter it because they had built it a little too high.'

'What about the old book, the one your father found in Japan? Do you know where it is? Perhaps that would help.'

Aimi went to the desk and came back with a large book that was so heavy she could hardly lift it. 'I always knew where it was, but I have never looked inside it. Perhaps I should now.'

The book looked very old. It was covered in red leather which was worn so thin that bits fell off as she handled it. She went back to the desk and returned with another, much smaller book. 'And this is my father's diary which I know he writes in every day.'

The big book was full of strange writings and drawings, none of which Dory could understand.

'This is written in ancient Japanese,' explained Aimi. 'It is very old and faded, which makes it difficult to read.' Carefully, they turned the pages, where now and then Aimi was able to make sense of the words. There were references to potions for all kinds of remedies – spells for good luck; how to predict the weather; the meanings of astronomical signs; herbal recipes; and even ways of making oneself invisible! So much information, thought Dory, it would take years to read it all.

Then Aimi opened the diary. There were entries in it right up to the morning of the day before. There was also a chart – a map of the world – tucked between the pages and this was marked with reference points in different areas. It also looked very old. Aimi turned back the pages of the diary until she came to a time when her father had discovered the old book. 'He says here,' she said, running her finger under the words, 'that on page 900 he found an account of some things called – well – the nearest thing in English, I suppose, would be "levels". As far as I can make out, these are places that exist alongside our own world, but we are unaware of them.'

She read on for quite a while, often very slowly because of the faded script and the old style of writing. 'These levels,' she continued at last, 'can be reached by any of the five *known* entrances that are marked on the map that was found between the pages of the old book.'

***

20

Together they spread out the map on the floor of the study. It showed the countries of the world as they must have been known then, not drawn as accurately as in a modern atlas, and with one or two countries missing. There were reference points, small arrows, in five different lands, each with a number written beside it. Aimi turned back to the diary.

'My father goes on to say that these arrows mark the places where, if the correct height can be reached, entry can be gained to that particular level. The correct height is the number beside the arrow.'

Neither of them spoke for a while as the words from the diary began to sink in, and then they looked at each other in astonishment. The tower! Was that why the Professor had built it, and to such an exact height? They looked at the map again, more closely now, until they found the location of the house where Aimi lived with her father, and there, in just the right place, they saw an arrow with a number written beside it.

Leafing through the pages of the diary, Aimi read of her father's growing excitement as he studied the old book and the map. Suddenly she came to a stop. 'I can't believe this,' she said, and she read aloud her father's account of what had happened a week before:

'Today I decided to enter the level marked on the old map. Aimi is quite happily playing in her room. If the book is correct, I shall be able to travel back and forth quite easily. I shall make a brief visit and should be back within half an hour.'

The Professor's diary continued:

'1.00 p.m. I went to the top of the tower and, not wishing to give myself time to have second thoughts, jumped off the platform. My immediate sensation was of slowly falling to the ground, but then I seemed to be moving sideways. How long I travelled so, I do not know. I then began to move downwards until at last I felt solid ground beneath me. Looking around, I saw that I was standing on a ledge on a cliff face. Close by was the mouth of a cave and in front of me was a path that led upwards. Below me and stretching away to the far horizon was a great ocean. I should have liked to explore further, but decided to return, not knowing how long the journey had actually taken. I then stepped off the cliff – not without some feelings of fear – and eventually found myself back on the tower. The clock in my study showed that I had been away for twenty-three minutes.'

Then Aimi turned the pages of the diary to yesterday's date:

'9.30 a.m. I shall make another brief journey to the "level". I am very keen to follow the path to the clifftop so that I may see what is up there. Once again, I shall return immediately.'

'Yesterday, after breakfast!' cried Aimi. 'Oh my poor father, what can have happened to him?'

She looked so sad that Dory was afraid that she was going to start crying again. Outside, he saw that the shadows had started to lengthen across the lawns. Soon his birthday would be over for another year. *His birthday!* He looked at the clock on the Professor's mantelpiece and suddenly realised that he would never be home in time for his birthday tea, even if he left now. Out of the corner of his eye he saw the worried look on Aimi's face, how she was biting her lip in an effort to stop herself from crying.

'How do you get up into the top of the tower?' he asked, quickly getting to his feet. 'Can we go there? We can't just sit here doing nothing.'

Aimi brightened a little and gave him a grateful smile. 'I have never been up there. But yes, I think we ought to take a look. The entrance is in the cellar. It is rather dark down there – I shall get a torch.'

***

Just one dim lightbulb lit the way as they made their way down a flight of stone steps and into the gloom. The cellar itself was in complete darkness and Dory wondered if Aimi's rather secretive father had deliberately kept it so. The base of the tower was at the far end of the room – a circular column of bricks with a shiny metal door that gleamed in the torchlight. There was no handle to be seen, but in the centre of the door was the design of a hand. Dory pressed his own hand against it, fully expecting the door to slide open, but nothing happened.

'This must be the way to open the door,' he said, 'or why would there be an outline of a hand?' He tried again, this time holding his hand against the design for several minutes, but it was no use. The door remained firmly shut.

Aimi had an idea. 'Let me try. Perhaps the door cannot be opened by strangers. As soon as she touched the hand, the door slid silently open.

'This house is full of surprises,' said Dory. 'Let's get in before it closes again.'

Once inside, they found that they were enclosed in a small metal cylinder – a kind of capsule – which had a row of buttons and dials on one side. A small green light came on as soon as the door had closed. They looked at the buttons and dials, but the only ones that made any sense to them were the ones marked 'Up' and 'Down'. Dory pressed the 'Up' button and they immediately found themselves moving smoothly upwards. He looked at Aimi, wondering if she also felt nervous, and was pleased to see that she looked quite calm. In a few seconds the capsule came to a halt and the door opened wide.

They stepped out into a little room that had a wide opening at one side. At the foot of the opening was a small step with a cross drawn in chalk upon it. The jumping-off spot, thought Dory. Looking down, he saw that directly below was a walled-in area, and piled up inside it was a heap of mattresses, perhaps as many as six or seven. The Professor had sensibly provided a soft landing for himself in case the information in the old book proved to be nothing more than a fairy story.

Aimi joined Dory at the opening. For a while they stood side by side in silence, neither of them knowing what to do or say next. At last Aimi spoke. 'He is my father, and I am going to see if I can find him. He writes about a cliff – perhaps he has fallen, had an accident, and is lying helpless. Yes, I am going, I have made my mind up. Please wait here for a while. If I do not come back soon, go home to your family.'

She took his hand and gave it a squeeze. 'You are a true friend,' she said, and I shall never forget you.' And then, before Dory could do more than make a grab for her sleeve, she jumped out of the opening. He watched as she disappeared – first her head, then her body and, finally, the soles of her shoes, just as though she had plunged into a pool of water.

***

Dory could not believe what he had just seen. A few seconds ago, Aimi had been standing next to him and now she was gone. It was one thing to read about travelling to another "level", or whatever it was called in the Professor's diary, but to see someone actually vanish into thin air – no, it wasn't possible! Dory looked down at the pile of mattresses, half expecting to see Aimi bouncing up and down and waving to him. But she seemed to have jumped completely out of sight. What she had just done was so unexpected that it left his mind in a whirl of uncertainty.

In the gardens below, nothing seemed to have changed, but what a day it had been! He had lost his kite, found it again, met a little Japanese girl whose father had gone off and left her on her own, and now she had vanished and left *him* on his own as well! When he had recovered a little, his first thought was to go after her. But what if something went wrong? What if he was unable to travel through whatever Aimi had just travelled through in the same way? But could he let her face things on her own in that strange place, or would he always regret it?

He looked down at the pile of mattresses and came to a sudden decision. At least he would have a soft landing if he didn't make it! He closed his eyes, crossed his fingers and took a deep breath. Here goes, he thought, as he sailed through the air and immediately began to fall.

Chapter 4

Dory had thought he was falling, but because there was nothing but empty space around him – no buildings or trees, or even clouds – it was difficult to tell. Next, he thought he must be moving sideways in a straight line and this sensation continued for a while until, with a jolt, he came to a stop and knew that he really was going downwards. Softly and slowly he floated down until, with not even the slightest bump, he felt solid ground under his feet.

He opened his eyes and looked around. Everything was just as the Professor had described it. There was the cave and the path that led up to the top of the cliff. Below him was a thin shoreline that edged along a great body of water, dark and waveless like a huge pool of oil that spread away as far as he could see. *But where was Aimi?* She wouldn't have ventured into the dark cave, he was sure. He began to climb the path. She couldn't have gone far in such a short time. Ah, Time! Was it the same in this place as it was at home? It seemed to be later in the day, although the lowering sun was still visible, its rays gliding across the flat ocean and colouring its surface with unnatural shades of turquoise and yellow.

The thought of spending a night in this unknown land filled him with unease. He had to find Aimi soon and try to persuade her to go back with him. Much to his relief, she hadn't gone far.

'Dory!' she cried, whirling around as she heard him scrambling over the top of the cliff. 'Oh, I am so glad to see you. I was feeling so lonely and afraid. Wherever are we?'

Dory didn't answer. He was too intent on watching two huge birds, as black as crows but very much bigger, that were flying straight towards them across the ocean.

'Quick!' he shouted, grabbing her by the hand. 'Come on! Run as fast as you can, back into the cave.'

Down the path they ran, stumbling and slithering in their hurry to get away, as they heard the 'whoosh' of the birds' wings and saw their giant shadows grow large across the face of the cliff beside them. Once inside the cave, they moved to the very back. One of the birds, its body blocking the whole entrance, poked its head inside, and they recoiled as the creature stretched its neck towards them as far as it could, its cruel beak snapping and striking out in frustration.

'Scare-*ree*!' cried Dory, twenty minutes later, when the big birds had finally left the cave entrance and had flown off across the ocean. 'Maybe coming here wasn't such a great idea!'

***

Slowly, he and Aimi crept out of the cave and looked fearfully around in case any other terrible creatures were about. He tried to think of what to say next in order to persuade Aimi to return home.

'Let us go up to the top again,' she suggested before he could speak. 'We did not really have time to look around properly.'

At the top of the cliff once more, they saw that they were in a meadow of tall grass that ran far away inland where patches of woodland, some no more than a dozen trees in size, grew wherever the ground rose up in little hills. The roots of every tree were huge and gnarled, clinging like tentacles to the sides of the ground wherever it was highest as though the trees were frightened of being blown away by the wind.

'I don't like the look of this place,' said Dory. 'I really think we should go home before it gets dark.'

Aimi agreed. 'Yes, but there do not seem to be any wild animals, or even any people about. Those big birds have gone, so do you think, perhaps, we could look just a little further?'

They walked along the clifftop for a while and then Aimi noticed that the grass ahead of them was flattened into a pathway as if it had been used a few times. Gradually, the path turned away from the cliff edge until it was leading quite directly inland.

'Perhaps this is the way my father came,' said Aimi, hopefully. 'Maybe we shall find a clue soon, something that will lead us to him.'

Dory said nothing. He didn't want to stray too far away from the spot where they had arrived, but also he didn't want to upset her. I'll wait until we get to that first clump of trees, he thought, and then I'll suggest that we should turn back. It was just then that they heard it. A sound that was not in the least bit loud but was very near. A small 'ping' that seemed to hover over them and then die away.

'What was that?' whispered Aimi as they stopped and looked at each other. Dory turned his head and listened, but now there was nothing but silence.

'I'm not sure,' he said quietly, 'but it sounded like – well – like a little bell.'

Then they heard it again. It *was* a bell, and now it continued, playing around their heads and making them think of sleigh bells at Christmas. Dory also remembered his first bicycle, which had a bell that rang just like it, and Aimi thought of her favourite toy, which was a music box that played a tune as a little ballerina twirled around on its lid. And, for the first time since their arrival, they both felt safe and comfortable, as if they were at home and lying in their beds.

'That was magical!' cried Dory, after the bell had stopped ringing. 'Let's go and see what's going on.' Together they crept towards the trees and then, seemingly out of nowhere, they heard a voice begin to sing:

'The Bellman rings his bell
To show that all is well,
So those who venture out at night
Will know that everything's all right.

And if they have no home,
They'll have no need to roam.
The Bellman always knows what's best –
He'll take them somewhere they can rest,
Ding-dong, ding-dong, ding-dong, ding-dong,
Just listen to the Bellman's song.'

Immediately the song had finished a tall figure stepped out from behind the trees. 'Hello, little friends! Don't be afraid. I'm the Bellman and I'm duty-bound to care for weary travellers. Please tell me – what are your names?'

The man wore a white robe and was carrying a lantern and a bell. He held the lantern up to his face and they saw that his hair and beard grew in tight little curls.

'Please sir,' said Dory, 'my name is Dory, and this is Aimi. We're looking for someone, but we haven't found them yet. So now we're going home and we'll come back tomorrow.'

The man came nearer with his lantern held high. 'But you're just children and in need of protection. Come, let me take you to a place, a kind place where you'll find food and a bed for the night.'

He waved the lantern around, revealing the twisted, snake-like roots of the trees that plunged through the undergrowth.

'There are wild creatures abroad at night,' he continued. 'See how the evening grows ever nearer. Come now and take rest, so that you may continue your search refreshed in the morning.'

He began to ring the bell once more. The children smiled at each other.

'He looks quite nice,' whispered Aimi. 'Shall we go with him?' But when they looked around, they saw that the Bellman was walking swiftly away.

'Wait!' called Dory. 'We're coming with you.' But the tall figure did not stop, or even look back, and soon he was completely out of sight.

'Come on,' cried Dory, 'we must catch him up. We'll have to follow the sound of the bell.'

***

It was now quite dark, but the clear notes of the bell still floated back to them as if to signal the way, and occasionally they caught glimpses of the lantern, now only a speck of light in the distance. The moon was no more than a sliver of light and they often stumbled over unseen roots and missed their footing on the uneven ground. Then, after perhaps half a mile, the sound of the bell stopped and the light from the lantern vanished from sight.

'We'd better keep going,' said Dory. 'Perhaps the Bellman has stopped for a rest and is waiting for us to catch up.'

They were now both very tired.

'I hope we soon find that place the Bellman talked about,' sighed Aimi, 'I would love to sit down for a minute – my legs are aching so much.'

Dory nodded. It had been a long day, or at least it felt like it had. So many strange things had happened that he seemed to have lost all sense of time. Then he felt Aimi tug at his sleeve.

'I think I can see a light ahead!' she cried.

Suddenly, out of the darkness, a voice boomed, 'Calling Miss Aimi and Master Dory!'

It wasn't the voice of the Bellman.

'Someone else knows our names,' commented Aimi. 'I wonder what they want with us.'

The light came from a large square building covered in climbing roses. *Welcome to the Rosegarden – a Rest for the Weary and the Poor –* read a sign above the door.

'Calling Miss Aimi,' cried the voice again. 'Has anyone seen Miss Aimi and Master Dory?' Suddenly, from behind them, a little man appeared. He was wearing a peaked cap and a green coat with brass buttons.

'Miss Aimi?' he asked and, turning to Dory, 'Master Dory, sir?' They both nodded. 'I've been looking for you everywhere. Come along now, everything is ready. One of the Bellmen has reserved your accommodation. Come along, please!'

Before they could speak, he hurried into the building, calling to them all the time over his shoulder, 'Come along, please!' Once inside, they were shown into a pleasant dining room, where a cheerful fire was burning brightly.

'Sit down wherever you like,' said the little man. 'Refreshments are on the way.'

Dory and Aimi looked at each other, as the same thought had occurred to them. 'You are very kind,' said Aimi, 'but I am afraid we have no money.'

'Money!' cried the little man indignantly. 'The Rosegarden doesn't take money from those in need!' He clasped his hands over his face and for a moment it looked as if he was going to cry.

'Money!' he repeated, raising his chin into the air. 'The very idea! Now you sit yourselves down while I fetch you some supper, and we'll say no more about it.'

'I hope we did not upset him,' whispered Aimi when he had gone, 'especially after he has shown us such kindness.'

But when the little man returned with a tray of sandwiches and two glasses of hot milk, he was all smiles. 'Eat up,' he said, 'then I'll show you to your beds.'

The thought of a cosy bed and a good night's sleep made Dory yawn. Soon Aimi was yawning too. 'Thank you,' she said when the man came to take away the tray. 'It was all very nice.'

'Yes,' agreed Dory, 'very nice.' He went on, 'Have you seen a man, a stranger, come this way recently? He's Japanese, like Aimi.'

'He is a professor,' Aimi added, 'and he would have been wearing a brown coat and trousers. Oh, and he wears his spectacles on the very end of his nose.'

The little man put his head on one side and thought for a moment.

'No-ooo,' he said slowly. 'We do get all sorts of folk passing through the Rosegarden, but I can't recall seeing that gentleman. Now, follow me up to your beds and then, if you wish, you can make an early start in the morning.' So saying, he led the way up a staircase in the corner of the room.

Suddenly, when they were nearly at the top, Dory thought that he saw the little man's body tremble and fade into just an outline for a second, before returning to normal just as quickly. I must be more tired than I realised, thought Dory, as he hesitated and rubbed his eyes before following the little man and Aimi to the top of the staircase.

***

They were shown into a room that had no windows, but was lit by a small piece of candle which was almost burnt out. By its light, they saw two single beds which seemed to be the only pieces of furniture in the room.

'Goodnight,' said the little man. 'See you in the morning.'

And, with that, he quickly closed the door and they heard the sound of a key being turned in the lock.

'He has locked us in!' cried Aimi. 'Why would he do that?'

Dory tried the handle of the door and nodded. Yes, they were locked in, but why?

They sat on one of the beds and looked around at the almost empty room. The walls were bare except for their shadows, which danced in the flickering light of the candle. It was all very different from the comfortable area they had just left.

'I am scared!' whispered Aimi. 'I wasn't before, but now I really, really am. What can we do?'

Dory was frightened as well, but he tried not to show it. 'Perhaps they always lock guests in at night, for their own safety.' He remembered how the little man had disappeared in front of him as they had climbed the stairs, and how he had put this down to his own tiredness. Was the little man a ghost? No, there had to be another explanation!

He tried again to open the door, but with no success.

'Hello,' he called out, 'is anyone there? Can you open the door, please? We don't like being locked in.'

But there was no reply, nor any other sound coming from the other side of the door. Worse was to follow. Much to their alarm they saw that the candle was now almost melted away and soon they saw the last bit of the wick go up in smoke.

'Oh, Dory,' cried Aimi, as they clung to each other in the darkness. 'I wish we had never come to this awful place!'

Chapter 5

For a while they said nothing as they became wrapped up in their own fearful thoughts, but they were glad of each other's silent closeness. Dory tried in vain to think of something he could say to comfort Aimi, but no words came. Was there a way to escape? The door was firmly locked and there were no windows, so there didn't seem to be much chance of that. In the stories he made up, there was always a way out. Either that or some hero would come dashing to the rescue. But this wasn't a story.

'Well,' he said at last, 'at least nothing's likely to happen until the morning, if that's any comfort. Let's try to get some rest. I don't suppose we'll go to sleep, but we might think of a way of getting out of here.'

'Dory,' whispered Aimi after a few minutes. 'Did you hear that? I think there is something in the room!'

Dory had heard it too – there *was* something, or some*one*, in the room – a wheezy, whispery sound, as if some kind of creature was having difficulty in breathing. And then the sound became words.

'Over here!' The voice was hoarse and sighing. 'I want to speak to you. Don't be afraid. Hurry up, there's not much time left!'

'The torch,' said Aimi, as she suddenly remembered it. 'The *torch*,' she hissed again, urgently. 'Have you still got the torch?'

Dory felt a wave of relief. The torch, which he had completely forgotten about, was still in his pocket. At least they wouldn't have to remain in this awful darkness.

The torch was small, but it had a powerful beam which he now shone in the direction from which the voice had come. At first he saw nothing unusual, but then he noticed a ripple of movement and saw to his surprise that the 'wall' was actually a long, dark curtain.

'Come closer,' said the voice. 'Don't be afraid. I'm a prisoner here, just like you. I want to help you.'

Just then a corner of the curtain lifted and a pale, bony hand appeared. 'Be quick,' said the voice, somewhat impatiently, as the hand beckoned them with a claw-like finger, 'unless you want to end up like me – left to die, empty, finished.'

Is this some new trick? Dory wondered, still on edge after all that had happened. 'Stay here while I take a look,' he said to Aimi. 'If there's any chance of getting out of here, we must take it.' But before he could move, Aimi grabbed his arm. 'No!' she said firmly, 'I shall come with you and hold the torch.'

Together they crept across the room and cautiously Dory pulled the curtain back a little. What they saw made them step back in fright. It was the gaunt, yellow face of an old man whose hair was white and uncombed.

'Aye,' said the man, in a quiet, sad voice. 'I suppose I must look like Death himself, but that's what happens to those who dance to the Bellman's tune.'

They saw that he was looking out at them from behind a row of iron bars that ran the full width of the room.

'Dowse your light, missy,' said the old man, 'so that we can talk in the dark, and keep your voices down.' He jerked his thumb over his shoulder. 'We mustn't wake any of the others. There's one or two who might shout out, and then all will be lost. The Massers will have you for sure.'

'Massers?' asked Aimi. 'Who are the Massers?'

'The Greymassers,' he replied. 'Now look, there's no time to prattle. You've got to get away from here as soon as you can. Listen carefully, the pair of you!' You're prisoners here. You're in the holding cell. The Rosegarden isn't real – it's a trick, a sham, a bit of jiggery-pokery. Your food has been doctored. You've been drugged to get you ready for tomorrow when they'll start their evil work on you – the first step to a lifetime of having the spirit drained from you, bit by bit.'

Aimi let out a gasp of terror and Dory felt her shiver in the darkness beside him.

'Don't take on,' said the old man quickly. 'All may not yet be lost.' He then began to cough, struggling to catch his breath, so much so that he had to hang on to the bars of the cell to keep from falling over.

'Worn out,' he gasped. 'Worn out before my time. But I'll get the better of them before I go – see if I don't! I'll not let them have their evil way with such as you. You're both young and healthy and that's in your favour. And you're not over-big, which is even better for what I have in mind.'

There was another pitiful fit of coughing which he tried his best to stifle for fear of raising the alarm. When he began to speak again his voice was even weaker than before but was filled with urgency.

'The gap between the last of these bars and the cell wall,' he rasped, 'is a bit wider than all the rest. I reckon you two should be small enough to squeeze through it. Then you must go very quietly past those poor souls who lie sleeping behind me – I'll lead you – and do the same at the gap at the far end. Then you'll find yourselves in the kitchen where they make up our grub, such as it is.'

Dory started to speak, but the old man held up his hand and shook his head. 'No time for questions,' he said, 'just listen. You'll see a door in front of you. It's not locked. Go through it and you'll be free. Then you must run for your very lives. Head down the valley. Just follow the stream until you come to the Great Thicket – that's a big parcel of dense forest – and get yourselves into it as deeply as you can. Then find a safe place to sleep off the effects of the vile stuff they've given you. I reckon you've got about an hour before it knocks you out completely. Now, let's try to get you away from here.'

Aimi went through the gap first, flattening herself against the wall and sliding through quite easily. Then it was Dory's turn. For several worrying minutes he became wedged in, unable to move either backwards or forwards, until at last with much pulling on his arm from Aimi and whispered instructions to breathe in he was able to wriggle free.

'Stay close behind me,' hissed the old man, as they crept slowly through the gloom, pausing now and then like statues whenever they heard a movement from one of the sleeping prisoners, and not daring to speak until finally they were through the bars at the far end of the room. Dory and Aimi turned to thank their benefactor, but he cut them short. 'Go now!' he urged. 'There's the door behind you. And remember what I told you!'

'What will happen to you?' asked Aimi, anxiously. 'Will you be in trouble for helping us?'

'Me?' said the old man. 'Well, I'm no use to them anymore and I haven't much time left. I don't fear them. If I've saved you, it'll all have been worthwhile, and I'll have had a bit of revenge!'

'Thanks for helping us,' whispered Dory. 'We'll never forget you. What's your name?'

There was a moment of silence and then the old man said sadly, 'I suppose I had a name once, but I seem to have forgotten it. Now go quickly, and good luck!'

Suddenly, as they turned to go, there was a noise – a kind of moaning sound from within the cell. Then the moan turned into a scream.

'Greymassers! Greymassers!' a voice wailed through the darkness. 'Come quickly! Someone's trying to leave, but it's not me, it's not me! Greymassers, come quickly!'

Soon more prisoners began to wake up, and the cell was filled with panic-stricken voices. 'It's not me!' they cried. 'It's not me! It's not me! It's not me!'

***

A welcome wave of fresh air greeted Dory and Aimi as they ran down the valley. The moon was high and they saw its bright image stretched in a thin line, shining along the length of the stream that would lead them down to the edge of the Great Thicket. Down and down they raced, through fields and over hedges, until the shouts of the prisoners faded to nothing more than a memory.

'Let us stop for a rest!' panted Aimi, after twenty minutes of hard running. 'Just let me get my breath back for a while.'

Dory, too, was glad to stop. His heart was racing and his lungs seemed to be on fire. They sank down on to the grass, but it was not long before they saw lights moving in the distance behind them and soon they were able to make out shadowy figures, crouched and scurrying like dogs, behind the swaying lanterns.

'They're after us!' cried Dory, springing to his feet. 'Why can't they leave us alone!' But Aimi was still out of breath and just shook her head as she got to her feet. Neither of them spoke again until they reached the edge of the Great Thicket.

'It looks a bit scary,' said Dory, as they looked up at the great wall of darkness, 'but we haven't any choice. We *have* to keep going!'

As soon as they entered the woods they found that running was no longer possible. The ground beneath the trees was covered in deep, thorny undergrowth that clutched at their clothes and scratched their legs. And the deeper into the woods they went, the darker it became. Using the torch would have been a great help, but they both agreed that it was far too risky. Soon they came to a place where the woods began to slope steeply away to one side, giving them a choice of direction.

'I think we should climb upwards,' said Dory. 'I know it'll mean harder going, but they'll surely expect us to take the easier way.'

But by now Aimi was truly exhausted. With her head hung down and her twig-filled hair across her face, she looked a sorry picture. Dory put his arm around her shoulders and gave her a squeeze.

'Come on,' he said. 'I'm sorry we have to keep moving. Let's hope we find a place to hide soon.'

***

It was only fear that had kept them going, but now a strange numbness began to creep through their arms and legs. Overhead, they saw the branches begin to weave spike-like patterns against the sky. The moon grew and shrank and then grew again into an enormous ball which burst and disappeared completely.

Suddenly, the sound of something crashing through the undergrowth startled them back to reality.

'Probably – badger – big – b-b-badger,' mumbled Dory, as speech now became more difficult. He took out the torch and shone it in the direction of the sound. It *was* a badger, and it was just about to disappear into a tunnel in the bushes, a well-used passageway with a floor of trodden ferns and a curved roof of leafy brambles. He found Aimi's arm and gave it a shake as he pointed the torch at the tunnel entrance.

'Sleep,' he said, drowsily. 'Sleep... in there!' Aimi nodded. Guiding her gently, he pushed her into the tunnel and crawled in after her. Deep inside they found a soft round nest of leaves, grasses and dried flowers that had obviously been used many times by some of the animals that lived in the woods.

'Nice,' murmured Aimi, who now seemed to be in a kind of dream-like state. Dory smiled and nodded. He couldn't believe their good fortune. It was an ideal spot in which to rest and they stood a very good chance of not being discovered. They had managed to do just what the old prisoner had advised. He lay down and closed his eyes. His arms and legs were scratched and had been stung by nettles and he was quite thirsty but at least he could now get some rest.

A soft cloud started to fall over him, covering him like a blanket. He began to dream that he was sinking into a deep pool of sunlit water where tiny red fish flashed and darted before his eyes and tall weeds rose to meet him, welcoming him to rest among them in the sandy depths. But, try as he might to reach the bottom of the pool, no matter how much he attempted to cling to the weeds, or dig fingers into the sand, something kept pulling him back. Some clear, voice-like music at the water's surface insisted on his return, until he gave up the struggle and allowed his body to float back up into the sunlight, to emerge gasping for breath and spitting the bitter taste of the water from his mouth.

Then it came to him – a faint tinkling sound that was the Bellman's enchanting tune; a song of home and comfort and happiness that they had followed so willingly before.

'*Come to me, come to me, there is no need to hide,*' it seemed to say. '*Follow the bell...*'

Aimi opened her eyes wide. 'It is the Bellman,' she whispered. 'Oh, Dory, it is the dear Bellman. He has come to take us home. Why ever did we run away from him?'

'Let's just listen to the music,' said Dory. 'That bell – I'm sure it's a magic one, and when the Bellman comes near we'll call out to him. Won't he be surprised!' They both then closed their eyes, so glad that the running was finally over.

Chapter 6

It was Dory who woke up first. He had been dreaming that he was at home, lying in his bed and listening to the birds singing outside his window. But his bed was not as comfortable as it should have been. It felt as if it was filled with hay and little twigs. And where were his bedclothes, and the steady ticking of the clock on his bedroom wall? Everything felt strange and he wondered if, perhaps, the answer was that he was not yet fully awake.

But there *were* birds singing, and they seemed to be perched somewhere above his head, where a bright light was filtering down through a swirling tangle of branches. Slowly he sat up and, as he did so, his head throbbed and felt as if it was about to split open and coloured lights flashed in front of his eyes. On top of all this, his mouth was full of a very nasty taste. Beside him he saw a little girl, who appeared to be asleep. On seeing her, he slowly began to remember the events of the day before – the Rosegarden, the kind prisoner, the chase and then the magical sound of the bell that had calmed their fears. And he recalled with a sharp pang of fright how much he had wanted to surrender to its beguiling music.

He turned to Aimi and called out softly, 'Wake up, Aimi, wake up.' When she showed no sign of stirring, he gave her arm a little shake and said, more loudly, 'Aimi, wake up, it's all right, we're safe now. Please wake up!'

It took several more minutes for Aimi to wake up and, as soon as she did so, she sat upright and gave a little scream of pain and alarm. Dory put his hand on her shoulder. 'Everything's all right,' he whispered reassuringly. 'We're safe and you needn't feel afraid.'

Like Dory, Aimi's head was aching and she, too, had a horrible taste in her mouth. They talked about what had happened to them the previous day and realised that not only had they been asleep for part of the night but, by the position of the sun, most of the morning as well. As their heads began to clear, they recalled, piece by piece, the events leading right up to the moment they had been about to fall under the Bellman's spell again.

'The drugs!' cried Aimi suddenly. 'It was the drugs that saved us.' On seeing the blank expression on Dory's face, she went on. 'The drugs must have taken effect just before the Bellman came too close. We must have been unconscious, so we could not respond to the bell. The drugs – their horrible drugs – they saved us!'

Dory nodded slowly. 'You're right,' he said, 'and to think he passed within a few feet of us!' They both shivered at the thought. 'Come on, we need to get away from here as soon as possible.'

Despite their ordeal, they both now felt a little more confident. The woods were full of sunlight and it seemed as though there was a singing bird in every tree. Slowly they pushed through the bushes until they were able to stand up. If it hadn't been such a trial, and so painfully close to the previous night's danger, they would probably have had a good laugh at each other. As it was, they each managed a wry smile. Their faces were streaked with mud and their hair was full of bits of twigs and leaves.

'We must find somewhere to clean ourselves up,' said Dory, 'and we need something to eat and drink to get rid of this awful taste.'

Aimi agreed. 'Whatever they put in our food,' she said, 'must have been really powerful. I still feel dizzy and my head is sore.'

They sat for a while in the sunshine and picked the bits out of each other's hair. Then they wiped their faces and hands with the long grass that grew in the shadows and was still damp with dew. The thought of going back to the cliff and travelling home, although very appealing, was soon dismissed when they remembered why they were here. Dory thought they should carry on.

'There must be someone who can help us,' he said. 'Let's see if we can find anyone.'

Aimi agreed. She thought about her father and wondered if she would ever see him again.

***

Although they were still deep in the woods, the trees were now further apart and the undergrowth was much less dense. Sometimes a rabbit jumped up and ran away as they approached and squirrels raced up into the treetops. Dory thought of the countryside at home and how, in many ways, this place resembled it. Soon, they came upon a little path. It was not much more than a track between the trees, but it was definitely a path that had been travelled on at some time. There were brightly coloured berries on the bushes that grew on either side but, hungry as they were, Dory and Aimi resisted the temptation to try them. Gradually, the path widened until it ran into a large clearing, and beside it they saw, to their surprise, a pleasant but overgrown garden in the middle of which sat a house.

Dory and Aimi watched for a while from a safe distance, wondering what to do next. They were desperate for food and drink, but they were scared that they might yet again fall into the clutches of the Bellman or some other awful creature who might wish to do them harm.

'It looks a very nice house,' commented Aimi, 'but almost as if it is deserted.'

Dory agreed. 'But we thought the Rosegarden was nice at first,' he added cautiously.

After much watching and whispering, hunger and thirst overcame their fear and they decided to take a closer look.

Dory and Aimi could see no one in the garden and the house showed no sign of being occupied. Curtains covered every window and the honeysuckle that was trained over the porch had now crept across the front door, attaching itself to the doorknocker and almost covering the letterbox. They tried to open the door, but it was locked. They looked at the windows, but they too were shut tight. They walked around to the back of the house, but the door there was also locked.

Dory felt a tug at his sleeve. 'Look,' said Aimi, pointing at the garden behind them. It was full of trees covered in fruit – apples, pears and plums hung from their sagging branches and some lay on the ground where they had fallen. Close by was an old iron pump with a water trough underneath. So they washed themselves and drank from it as they took it in turns to pump the handle. Then they sat under the trees and feasted on the juicy fruit as they dried themselves in the sunshine.

They looked at the house again. 'There is probably not another house for miles,' said Aimi. 'This would be a good place for us to stay for the night. We could get a proper rest and decide what to do in the morning. It is obvious no one lives here anymore.'

'Well,' said Dory rather doubtfully, 'it's all securely locked. I wouldn't like to break any of the windows to get in. It must belong to somebody.'

Aimi had an idea. 'I wonder if...?' she started to say, and then changed her mind. 'Let us go round to the front again,' she suggested. 'I want to try something.'

Dory followed her as she hurried around the house where she began to pull some of the honeysuckle away from the door.

'I hope I shall be lucky,' she said, as she pushed open the flap of the letterbox. 'And I am!' she exclaimed. 'Just hold the flap open for a while. I think I have found the key.'

Moments later, she was pulling up a long piece of string from inside the house and on the end of it was a large key.

'When we lived in Japan,' she explained, 'my father, who is very forgetful, was always losing the front door key. So he used to keep a spare one hanging behind the letterbox. I would guess that whoever lived here had the same problem!'

'We're in!' cried Dory, as she turned the key in the lock. 'You *are* clever! I'd never have thought of that in a hundred years.'

Long strands of cobweb brushed across their faces as they entered the hallway and spiders scuttled away from the sudden intrusion of light. There was a cupboard in the kitchen containing a few crumbs of bread and some stale cheese that had been nibbled by mice, and on a small table was an empty plate and a spoon. A pot plant that had died from a lack of water stood, brown and shrivelled, on the windowsill.

'Someone liked nice things,' said Aimi, as they explored the rest of the house. There was comfortable, ornate furniture in every room and thick, colourful rugs covered most of the floor. It was obvious that no one had lived here for quite a while, but why, they both wondered, would anyone go off and leave it all behind?

'We have to make a plan,' said Dory, 'as to what we should do tomorrow.' He tried to sound hopeful, but in his heart he felt anything but. They had to get home, but how? There was also the Professor to think of. They hadn't seen or heard anything of him, and where could they possibly start to look? He could be anywhere. He could even be – well, Dory tried to put that possibility out of his mind.

'This looks like a nice room,' said Aimi, as they passed an open doorway. 'Let's sit in there. Despite the lack of light, they could see that this was where meals were taken. There was a long dining table in the centre of the room, complete with chairs for four people. The walls were hung with ancient-looking weapons — swords, shields and daggers, and in one corner was a suit of armour that had fallen down into a heap. They sat at the table and tried to decide on their next move.

***

'It is so gloomy in here,' said Aimi after a while, getting to her feet. 'Perhaps we could think more clearly if we let some light in.' She peered around the side of the heavy curtains and looked out for a few minutes. 'I do not think there is anyone about,' she added as she pulled the curtains back, 'but we should stay away from the window for safety's sake.'

The sunlight swept into the room, lighting every dark corner and lifting Dory's worried mood. He looked around and, for a while, he forgot about the danger they were in as he tried to imagine who had once lived in the house and had sat at the table, as he was doing now. Someone adventurous, perhaps, going by the swords and armour. There was a large painting hanging over the mantelpiece. It was a portrait of an old gentleman with grey, curly hair, side-whiskers and rosy cheeks, but he didn't look very adventurous. He was smiling and his eyes twinkled out from behind his spectacles. He looked more like Father Christmas than a soldier!

They began to talk about what they ought to do next. Should they return to the cliff and try to get home? The threat of the Bellman and returning to the Rosegarden filled them both with fear. And what of Aimi's father? He was still missing.

'We could travel at night,' he said, 'and try to avoid those awful creatures.'

Aimi didn't reply. She just nodded slowly and he saw that her eyes were filled with tears.

'Who knows,' he went on quickly, 'perhaps your father has returned home and is now wondering where you are?' The thought was worrying and they agreed that they should have left a note behind.

The afternoon sun still filled the room with its warm rays and soon they began to yawn, as their recent exertions started to catch up with them. There was a comfortable settee at the end of the room, and there they sat for a while, saying nothing and enjoying, if only for now, being free from the strange creatures who were intent on catching them.

***

It was Aimi who heard it first. 'What was that?' she said, suddenly sitting upright and looking around the room.

'What was what?'

'That funny sound – a kind of squeak. Surely you must have heard it!'

Dory shook his head. 'It was probably a mouse,' he said. 'We have them in *our* old house. They're quite harmless, but they can be a bit of a nuisance.'

Then the sound came again, and this time Dory heard it as well. 'These old houses...' he began to say, but before he could finish the sentence they saw, to their amazement, that the suit of armour had begun to move! Twitching and jerking, creaking and clanking, the legs and arms began to bend, straighten, and bend again, until the whole suit stood in front of them in a shower of dust.

Dory wanted to get up and run to the far end of the room, but his legs refused to move. Aimi was the same – fixed to the spot in fear and wonder as they sat quite still in open-mouthed disbelief. Then, to their astonishment, the figure began to speak.

'Please do not be alarmed,' said a voice from inside the armour, 'I mean you no harm. You are perfectly safe.'

The voice was pleasantly soft and gentle, not at all what one would expect from a figure in full armour. Then the visor at the front of the helmet lifted and a pair of the bluest eyes either of them had ever seen gazed out at them, eyes that looked as though they had been made from pure crystal.

'I see before me,' the voice continued, 'a pair of children, one male and one female. My name is Sir Kitry. Please be kind enough to introduce yourselves.'

Chapter 7

Dory spoke first. 'Please, Sir Kitry,' he began, when he had recovered a little from his shock. 'M-m-my name is Dory and this is Aimi. We didn't mean to break into this house. Well, we didn't really break in. We used a key that was tied to a piece of string ... and we had nowhere else to stay ... and we were looking for someone ... and we seem to be lost ... and please help us if you can!' And then, perhaps because of the presence of this being who, despite its strange appearance, sounded so calm and kind and not at all frightening, all the dangers that they had faced so recently seemed to overwhelm him. He suddenly felt small and helpless and lay back in his seat, looking at Aimi. 'We need someone's help,' he said, pitifully. 'We don't know what to do next.'

Aimi agreed. 'Yes, yes,' she cried. 'We have been given nasty food by the Grey-somebodies, and chased through the woods by the Bellman. Oh, you are not anything to do with them, are you? Please say you are not!'

On hearing this, Sir Kitry's head shook vigorously from side to side and his visor jumped up and down. 'Oh no – no, no, no!' he exclaimed. 'Nothing of the kind. I am a knight, a long-standing member of the Noble Order of the Loyal Protectors.' He stood to attention. 'Sir Kitry,' he added, briskly. 'Serial number zero, nine, nine. Manufactured by Zimco's Limited as a very special order for Doctor Hugo Batram, a respected physician of the south-west section of the country of Pellagaroo.' He sat down and bowed his head. 'The late Doctor Hugo,' he continued, with a little choke in his voice, 'whose house you are now occupying.'

There were questions that both Dory and Aimi wanted to ask, but Sir Kitry sat with his head lowered for such a long time that he seemed to have fallen asleep. Then, just when Dory had plucked up the courage to say something, the knight lifted his head.

'Forgive me,' he said quietly. 'It seems that I am not quite back to my old self yet. Now, where was I?'

'Doctor Hugo?' asked Aimi. 'You were telling us about Doctor Hugo.'

'So I was!' exclaimed Sir Kitry, 'but look, suppose we sit down together and you tell me about your troubles. Then I shall see if I can help you. It is the least I can do, seeing that you have brought me back to life.'

The children looked puzzled. 'Brought you back to life?' asked Dory, 'I don't understand.'

'Of course you don't. I should have explained. I am – well – the old-fashioned term would be a 'robot', I suppose, although we knights do not really like using that word. We are much, much more than that. Unlike our robotic ancestors, we have the ability to think for ourselves. We are also endowed with feelings. We know sadness, happiness, humour and compassion – in fact, we are very much like you humans, except that we are not flesh, blood and bone, but a collection of valves, wires and chemicals enclosed in a metal structure. I am proud to call myself one of Zimco's top models!'

'Of Zimco's Limited?' asked Aimi, remembering what he had said earlier.

'Exactly so,' said Sir Kitry. 'Yes, indeed. I am one of Zimco's children.'

The knight spread his arms wide and let the remains of the day's sunshine gleam across his chest.

'Power from the sun,' he explained, 'or even just daylight. That is what keeps me going, and very long periods without it will deprive me of my existence. I am *solar-powered*, you see. It must have been you children who pulled back the curtains and let the sunshine in.'

He rubbed his chest.

'Ah,' he sighed, 'I feel better already, but it is all my own fault that I collapsed in such a silly fashion. *Emotion* – that was the cause of it. Sometimes I think I would be better off without it!'

He pointed at the portrait.

'There he is,' he said, 'my late employer and friend. Doctor Hugo was a delightful man. I was his companion and, I am proud to say, his guardian for many years. We went for walks together, played chess – sometimes I let him win!' He chuckled at the memory and continued, 'I even helped him tend the fruit trees, which, judging from the juice stains on your faces, you seem to have found already!'

'But where is he?' asked Aimi. 'Why are you alone in this house?'

Sir Kitry got up and stood in front of the doctor's portrait. 'One day,' he said, sadly, 'he did what all humans eventually do – he passed away. He is buried in the back garden. I laid him there myself beneath his favourite tree. Then I came back into the house, drew all the curtains, sat in the corner and let my batteries fade away. What a silly thing to do, not what he would have wanted at all!'

***

Nothing was said for a while. The children realised how sad the knight must have been and neither of them could think of what to say to comfort him.

'Just listen to me!' he exclaimed, as he returned to his chair. 'Sharing my sorrows with you when I should be trying to help you. You had better start by telling me how you came here. You sound and look like newcomers.'

'We are,' said Dory. 'You won't believe this, but we jumped off a tower and found ourselves in this strange place.'

Sir Kitry didn't seem at all surprised by this information. 'Tell me,' he said, 'where exactly did you arrive? Can you describe it?'

'It was on the side of a cliff,' replied Dory, 'near a cave.'

'And a great ocean that seemed to stretch away forever,' added Aimi.

The knight's visor jumped up and down and he said, 'Entry number five! I know it well. You must have travelled through channel number three.'

He put his head on one side and looked at them with eyes that seemed to shine more brilliantly than ever. 'I have much information stored away in here,' he said, tapping his head. 'I am not just an old tin can, you know!'

He seemed to find what he had just said highly amusing and began to laugh as though he was never going to stop, his eyes rolling around so swiftly that they became a blur of blue light. He looked so comical that soon Aimi and Dory were laughing as well. Their laughter eventually died down. 'We come from Earth,' said Dory, 'and we don't really know where we are now.'

Sir Kitry shook his head. 'You have much to learn,' he said. 'Too much for such young heads to take in all at once, but I can assure you that you are still on Earth. But you are not on – how shall I put it – your version of it. The universe seems to be composed of many layers or "levels" as some people like to call them. This level, where you are now, is separated from yours by hardly more than the thickness of a piece of paper. Those who arrive at this level either do so by accident – they "fall through the hole", as we say, or by design – in other words, they have discovered the means of getting here. Tell me, please, what brought you here?'

Listening to these words, Dory saw that the Professor's old book was beginning to make sense. He looked at Aimi and saw that she was nodding her head. It was time to tell their new friend everything that had happened to them.

***

'Well,' said Sir Kitry, 'you have had a dreadful time. This can be a very dangerous place to wander about in, right up to the Nine Peaks, although I have never travelled that far myself.'

'You mean because of the Greymassers and the Bellmen?' asked Aimi, as she peered anxiously out of the window.

'Not just them. There are some wild animals that are best avoided, and, as for the grizlings – those birds that attacked you – well, they are truly dreadful creatures, pets of the Blaggards, no less, who are just as awful.'

The sun was now falling behind the trees and the room gradually filled with shadows. 'Will you be all right,' asked Dory, 'now that the light's fading?'

Sir Kitry got to his feet and nodded. 'Oh yes,' he said, 'I have had a good top-up of sunshine and tomorrow shall have some more. Now, let us cheer this old room up a little.'

Wood and coal were already laid in the fireplace and soon they were blazing and crackling, filling the room with a welcome glow.

'This place, the country of Pellagaroo,' explained Sir Kitry, when he had settled down into one of the big armchairs, 'was once populated entirely by humans. Oh, there were animals, of course, and birds – in fact, it was probably much like the level on which you live, but not necessarily of the same time period. Newcomers arrived from all parts over the years, mostly by accident. They had no means of returning home and didn't really know how they got here, so most of them settled down and raised families. Many brought new skills and helped the country to develop and flourish. But then the Greymassers arrived and everything changed.'

'Who are they?' asked Aimi, unable to contain her curiosity.

'Yes, and where do they come from?' added Dory.

Sir Kitry got up and closed the curtains, and when he returned, his eyes reflected the fire's red glow. 'You must understand,' he said, 'that all this happened before I was created. And the truth is that no one knows the answers to those questions. What *is* known is that they are grey and shapeless, but are able to assume any form that suits them at any particular time. My guess is that they came creeping and slithering through the levels. What we also know is that they need a constant supply of human victims in order to survive. I'm not sure of the exact details. Only those unfortunate prisoners that you saw will know those. But once they have you in their power, they connect themselves to you in some horrible way and transfer your human life-force. Without that daily supply of human spirit they would just fade away.'

'Those poor prisoners,' sighed Aimi, 'and that brave old man. Just think what would have happened to us without his help!'

'And the Bellmen,' asked Dory, 'are they the Greymassers' servants?'

Sir Kitry considered the question. 'I am not sure that they are actually servants,' he said. 'They certainly do the Greymassers' dirty work for them, roaming the countryside looking for victims. Some folk say that they are Greymassers themselves, in one of their many guises. They *can* be evaporated, so that proves that they are without any real substance. So, maybe they are. They are certainly just as evil!'

He got up and stretched his arms. 'I am still a little on the stiff side,' he said, 'but tomorrow I should be fine.'

He piled more coal on the fire. 'There, that should last until morning. I suggest you curl up where you are and get some sleep. The beds upstairs are not aired, but I am sure you will be just as comfortable down here.'

Aimi began to yawn. 'You said that the grizlings were the pets of the Blaggards,' she said drowsily. 'What are the Blaggards?'

'Yes,' added Dory, 'and what did you mean by "evaporated"?'

Sir Kitry shook his head. 'Tomorrow,' he said. 'You have had enough to worry about for one day.'

Chapter 8

When they awoke the next morning, Dory and Aimi found two bowls filled with blackberries waiting for them on the kitchen table. Aimi looked out of the window and was relieved to see the knight sitting in the garden.

'There was no food in the house,' he said when they joined him,' so it was only nature's harvest for breakfast, I am afraid. No substitute for eggs on toast, I am sure, but at least you will not starve.'

As Dory and Aimi thanked him, he continued, 'I have been thinking about what to do next. We know that Aimi's father arrived here, but we do not have any idea where he is now. I think it is time we went to call on my friend, Sir Mons, otherwise known as Captain Coaleye.'

'Captain Coaleye!' exclaimed Dory.

'Yes, he lives at Castle Gardemal. It is the headquarters of the Loyal Protectors and the place where our maintenance work is now done.' The knight stretched his arms and legs. 'I need a bit longer in the sun and then I shall be back to my full strength.'

'Tell us about the Loyal Protectors,' said Aimi, while they waited for the knight to warm up. 'Are they knights like you?'

Sir Kitry, who had been sitting in a relaxed way, almost dozing, now sat upright. 'Yes they are,' he replied. 'My dear comrades and I are all knights, ever ready to defend the good citizens of Pellagaroo. After the Greymassers came, the peaceful and happy life of the people ceased to be. A sombre cloud seemed to cover the land. Folk were afraid to venture out for fear of being lured into their clutches. Everyone hated the Greymassers and the Bellmen, but no one could think of a way to defeat them. They were like will-o'-the-wisps, phantoms, clouds – when you tried to tackle them, you found that they had no substance. Things became so bad that the senior members of the community got together to try to find a solution. Then, one day, someone remembered Signor Zimco.'

'Was he a clever man?' asked Dory.

'He was a genius, a brilliant scientist and engineer who was a leading figure in the field of robotics and – a term I do not much like – artificial intelligence. When and how he arrived here I do not know, but I am so very glad that he did because he brought all those skills with him.'

'And it was his idea to make beings such as you to guard people?' asked Aimi. 'To protect them from the Greymassers?'

'Exactly so. That is why he made us all knights, so that we would always remember our duty to protect the weak. The demand for knights became so great that he set up in business and soon almost every household had one or more of its own.'

He patted his chest and stood up. 'I think I am back to full power, but we shall just try a little test to check.' He raised his right arm. 'Long live the Loyal Protectors,' he proclaimed, and as he did so a thin line of red fire shot out of his forefinger and up into the air.

'What the... what on earth was that?' exclaimed Dory.

Sir Kitry showed them his finger, which was still glowing slightly, and they saw that there was a hole at the tip of it.

'Firepower,' he said, 'courtesy of Signor Zimco. And that is how we evaporate the Greymassers and their dangerous friends. The snag is, though, they somehow manage to re-form themselves after a few hours. Come on, let us lock up the house and set off for Castle Gardemal.'

***

The path away from the house soon became wider until they were able to walk at an even pace, unhampered by branches and undergrowth. Birds sang above their heads and now and then clouds of multi-coloured butterflies, of a kind they had never seen before, rose up as they passed by. Were it not for the worry about Aimi's father and the situation they were in, it would have been very pleasant, but the thought of what might lie ahead was constantly on their minds.

'You were going to tell us about the Blaggards,' said Aimi, 'whatever they are. They do not sound very nice. Why would anyone want to keep those awful grizling birds as pets!'

'I was rather hoping you were not going to ask me about them,' replied Sir Kitry, 'at least not yet. But they could be – and I stress *could* be –involved in your father's disappearance. Did you say he was a professor, a scientist of some kind?'

'Oh, yes,' said Aimi, proudly, 'and much more besides. He is also a very successful inventor.'

Sir Kitry shook his head. 'Just the kind of person the Blaggards like to get their hands on, especially if they thought he could provide them with firepower.'

On hearing this, Aimi let out a gasp of dismay.

'Please don't cry,' said Sir Kitry, patting her on the shoulder. 'Remember that I am going to help you as much as I can.'

'I am all right,' said Aimi. 'It is better to know the facts. Please tell us about them.'

Sir Kitry sat down on a nearby tree stump and the children flopped down on the grassy patch that had grown around it.

'The Blaggards are a very bad lot,' he recounted, 'but it is not entirely their fault that they turned out to be so wicked. You see, a considerable number of the early models of the Loyal Protectors passed through the production line without being wired up correctly. Some of the most important qualities that we are required to possess – honour, for instance, and compassion, loyalty, kindness, happiness, and even sadness – were left out. It was all a terrible mistake. Poor quality control, of course. But before they could be recalled for remodelling it was too late. They had all gone off together and formed a rebellious alliance. They painted their armour black and called themselves the "Black Guards". This has been changed by the rest of us over the years to "Blaggards".'

He stopped, and his eyes, usually so bright, began to lose some of their colour. Was he really back to his full strength, wondered Dory, or perhaps just sad because someone had made a mistake? Sir Kitry stood up. 'Come on, or all the food will have gone. I can talk as we go.' But it was several minutes before he resumed his story.

'The poor Blaggards,' he sighed. 'Yes, they are poor in the things that really matter. Their aim is to take over the country, but luckily for us they were never fitted with firepower. They have to resort to brute force, using old-fashioned weapons – swords, crossbows and the like.'

'Where do they live,' asked Dory. 'Do they have a castle?'

'They have a stronghold somewhere up in the Nine Peaks. We do not know exactly where. Rumour has it that it is on the far side. We think that is where they take their captives – clever people who can make them more powerful and others who they use as general workers, no more than slaves really. The worst Blaggard of all is their leader, General Madza. He's to be avoided at all costs!'

***

It was past midday before the castle came into view. The woodland path had ended rather abruptly and they were suddenly aware of a threshold of bright light ahead.

'There,' Sir Kitry pointed as they stepped out of the shadows, 'do you see it? There, at the top of that hill?

That is Castle Gardemal where we shall find the mighty Sir Mons and his men.'

Below them they saw a large, flat-bottomed valley where masses of blue flowers formed a patchwork in the fields and herds of deer grazed under sturdy trees. Rising up from the valley floor was a large hill crowned with the castle, a square building with a turret at each corner, each bearing a long golden pennant that furled and unfurled in the breeze.

'It looks very peaceful,' commented Dory.

'Yes,' agreed Aimi, 'just like a castle in a fairy story.'

'It does,' said Sir Kitry, 'and it is probably the safest place in the whole country. And that is because it is the home of the Loyal Protectors, of whom Sir Mons is one of the longest-serving members.'

'Captain Coaleye?' asked Dory. 'Why do you call him that?'

There was a glint of sunlight on glass from the castle battlements. Sir Kitry laughed. 'The telescopes are out, so they will be expecting us. Come along and you can see for yourself!'

Dory didn't have long to wait for an answer to his question. As they approached the castle they saw a giant figure in armour striding towards them.

'Hail, strangers! Do you come in peace? And you, Sir Knight, are you loyal or will you face Sir Mons in deadly combat and end your days in the Great Scrapyard?'

The children looked anxiously at Sir Kitry. 'Do not worry,' he said quietly, 'he knows it is me – he is just having some fun with us.'

'Hail Brother,' he shouted back, 'I come in peace. I am loyal. Here's fire to your forefinger!'

There was laughter, and a great rumbling roar of delight from Sir Mons, and soon he was embracing Sir Kitry, lifting him off the ground and causing sparks to fly from their breastplates as they clashed together.

'*This* is Sir Mons,' Sir Kitry told the children, when he had been released and set back on his feet.

'Hello, Sir,' said Dory, politely. 'I'm Dory and this is Aimi. It's nice to meet you.'

Sir Mons bent down and they saw that, while one of his eyes was blue, the other was as black and shiny as a piece of coal.

'Do you know what they call me?' he asked.

'C-C-Captain C-Coaleye, sir?' stuttered Dory.

Sir Mons stood up and placed his hands on his hips. 'What impudence!' he bellowed. 'Just for that I shall take you back to my castle and have you for my supper!'

With that, he picked up both Dory and Aimi and carried them off under his arms, where they kept very quiet and still, hoping with all their hearts that it was all just a joke. After all, robots didn't eat *anything*, did they?

***

Once they were inside the castle gates, Sir Mons put them gently down. 'I have changed my mind,' he said. 'I am not going to eat you. Why, there is not enough meat on you to feed a mouse!'

He turned to Sir Kitry. 'Well, Kit, judging by the appearance of your little companions, I guess we have much to talk about.' He looked Sir Kitry up and down. 'I hope you don't mind me saying so, but you look as if you could do with a bit of a clean-up yourself. I shall take you over to the finishing shop, if you like, for an oil and polish. We cannot go letting the Loyals down, can we?'

He beckoned the children to follow him and led them through a courtyard and into a large kitchen where they were surprised to see about a dozen humans eating a meal at a long table.

'Here are two hungry travellers, Mrs Bonny,' he said to a woman wearing an apron and a chef's hat. 'I think they may be visitors from the Other Side. Show them how we treat guests in Pellagaroo, if you please.'

Soon Dory and Aimi were enjoying a delicious meal of roast venison and dumplings with plenty of vegetables and hot, spicy gravy. Even though they both tried their best, for the sake of good manners, not to gobble too quickly, their plates were soon empty.

'Why, you're half-starved, 'said Mrs Bonny as she refilled their plates. 'Eat up now. There's plenty more where that came from.'

There were smiles of welcome from the others at the table, each of whom wore a set of blue overalls.

'Hello,' said a young man who didn't look much older than they were. 'My name's Gully. I haven't been working here long. I'm following the family tradition. My father worked at the old Zimco factory. He was a sheet metal worker and that's what I'm training to be.'

He waved his hand around the table. 'Most of the others do more of the technical work with brain circuitry, joint mechanics, visual and hearing operations and so on. We're all part of the team that keeps the knights maintained and repaired.'

'Like a hospital for robots?' said Aimi.

The young man smiled. 'Yes, but we try not to use the "R" word here,' he whispered. The children looked puzzled. 'The knights are a bit sensitive about being called "robots" and we don't want to upset them, do we!'

***

When the meal was over, Gully offered to show them around the castle. They began with the workshops.

'It's strange to think that Sir Kitry is full of all this machinery – wires, cogs and stuff,' said Dory, as they watched a head being rebuilt. 'He seems so human, doesn't he?'

'He does,' replied Gully, 'and in many ways he is, as are all the Loyal Protectors. Yes, these knights are truly amazing.' He picked up a metal hand and moved the long fingers up and down. 'A hand like this can crush a thick piece of wood into splinters or pick up a butterfly by its wings without harming it.'

They moved through storerooms and peered into little rooms where voice boxes were being assembled and eyes were being cut from lumps of crystal rock. Gully opened a door marked with the letters 'D.W.' 'Damaric Water,' he explained, 'though I believe it's actually an oil. Named after one of Signor Zimco's team who discovered it many years ago.'

Before them they saw some large glass tanks full of a golden liquid that swirled slowly around as if it was being stirred by an unseen force.

'It scares me a bit,' said Gully. 'It seems to have a life of its own, but I know that's not really possible. Anyway, it proved to be the breakthrough the team was hoping for. I suppose it works a bit like our blood.' His shoulders twitched and a shiver ran through his body. 'My old dad always used to say it was the thing that turned machines into men.'

He closed the door. 'Let's go up top and get some fresh air.' "Up top" proved to be the roof of the castle, a flat area surrounded by stone battlements and overlooked by a tower at each corner.

'What a view!' exclaimed Aimi, as she stood on her toes to peer over the wall. 'And all those blue flowers. There must be millions of them.'

Gully pointed at the long pennants fluttering in the breeze. 'Part of our national emblem,' he said, 'embroidered on our very own flag. Long may it fly!'

He smiled at the children. 'There's still much more to see, but I have to get back to work. You can stay here until Sir Kitry returns, if you like. I'll tell him where you are. It'll be time for firepower practice soon. You'll get a good view of it from here. Just don't lean too far out over the wall!'

'Firepower practice!' said Dory, after Gully had left. 'That sounds interesting.'

They looked out at the landscape, gazing at the green meadows, white-walled cottages and farmhouses that were so similar to those at home, but much further apart from each other.

'It all looks so peaceful,' said Aimi, 'but so many bad things are going on.' She covered her face with her hands. 'My father is somewhere out there. Oh, Dory, where can he be?'

Dory turned and put his arm round Aimi's shoulders. 'Please don't worry. We'll find him,' he said, gently. 'We have some good friends now who are going to help us. And then we can all go home.'

***

The welcome sound of laughter from below quickly raised their spirits as a group of knights assembled for firepower practice. Balloons were released and powerful red streaks of light came flashing upwards, accompanied by cheers every time a balloon was destroyed or laughter each time the target was missed. It was a good demonstration of what an effective weapon the Loyal Protectors possessed and how skilful they were at using it. No wonder the Blaggards were desperate to get their hands on it.

'How lucky we are,' said Dory, 'to be in such good company. I've got a feeling that everything's going to be all right.'

Aimi smiled and nodded. Then Sir Kitry came marching across the courtyard below, his head held high and his step as brisk and measured as a soldier's.

'Ah, there you are,' called the knight, as he came bounding up the steps. 'Did you enjoy the display?' He looked very alert, his eyes were bright and his newly polished armour shone like gold in the last rays of the setting sun.

On the opposite side of the battlements stood a single figure, a knight who now began to beat on a drum, slowly and solemnly, as four other knights slowly lowered the pennants.

'This happens every evening at sunset,' Sir Kitry explained, 'but they will be raised again at first light. After that you must have some breakfast and then we must be on our way.'

'Where are we going? asked Aimi. 'Is it very far? How will we get there?'

Sir Kitry took her by the hand and led them both into one of the turrets and up a stairway to the top. 'There,' he pointed, 'do you see those mountains in the distance that look a bit like a row of teeth?'

The light was fading, but they could just make out the jagged outline of a mountain range.

'Those are the Nine Peaks where the Blaggards have their stronghold. Somewhere up there is where they take their prisoners.'

'Is that where my father is?' cried Aimi. 'Please tell me the truth!'

Sir Kitry put a hand on her shoulder. 'Be brave, but yes, he almost certainly is. Word has reached us that two Blaggards were seen to ride off with a man who fits your father's description.'

There was a cry of despair from Aimi and, however much she tried not to cry, her eyes filled with tears.

Dory tried to soften the bad news. 'They probably won't harm him, will they, as long as they believe he can be useful to them?'

Sir Kitry patted him on the back. 'Well put. No, they will certainly not harm him, but they will treat him as a prisoner. Another good thing is that we have an agent – a spy – among them. He joined the Blaggards a long time ago to gain a position of trust until an opportunity arose to bring them down. To be honest, we have not heard from him since the day he joined them, but that is to be expected. He will certainly help the Professor if he can.'

'Is he a Loyal Protector, like you?' asked Aimi.

Sir Kitry nodded. 'He is, and a very brave one. He carries no firepower, for that would give the game away. His armour is black, and we do not know what name he has adopted. But he has one distinguishing feature – a scorch mark on his right arm to pretend that he has had a brush with our firepower.'

'What would happen to him if he was found out?' asked Aimi. 'Would they punish him?'

Sir Kitry hesitated. 'They would show him no mercy,' he replied. 'He would be hurled off one of the highest peaks to smash into little pieces on the rocks below – so many pieces that it would be impossible to put him back together again.' He paused for a moment with his head on one side. 'Not even by all the king's horses and all the king's men.'

'Humpty Dumpty!' exclaimed Dory. 'Who told you about him?'

The knight shook his head. 'I do not know,' he said wonderingly. 'How very strange. I really do not know.'

Chapter 9

It was the sound of the drum once again that roused Dory the following morning, but this time the beat was much faster. It seemed to bring an urgency to the start of the day and, by the time he looked out of his window, the flags were hoisted and the drummer was gone.

His bedroom was at the rear of the castle and here he could see that the blue flowers grew more thickly than ever, smothering all but a few patches of green. A slight breeze stirred the flower heads into wave after wave of movement, reminding him of his home at the foot of the high moors where the heather often moved in just such a way.

A knock on the door interrupted his thoughts and he heard Aimi telling him she was up and dressed and that she would see him at breakfast. The sound of her voice cheered him, but he realised how sad she must be too. Not only was she also away from home, but her father was a prisoner of the terrible Blaggards. This was no time to be homesick, he told himself, and he put the sad thoughts out of his mind.

Sir Kitry joined them as they ate their breakfast. 'Our plan,' he said, as he pulled up a chair and sat down, 'is for Sir Mons and myself to go up into the mountains and search for the Blaggards' headquarters.'

Dory raised a hand. 'How will you know where to look?' he asked. 'Those peaks stretch for miles.'

'Good question,' replied Sir Kitry, 'but local legend has it that there is only one way up from this side. It's at the base of the sixth peak from the left, the one shaped like a dog with its nose in the air. If the Blaggards go back and forth from here to their fortress, as we know they do, they must have to take that track.'

One of the kitchen staff came out to clear away the dishes and, after she had gone, Aimi had a question. 'Surely some of the people who live here know someone who has been up into the mountains – an older relative perhaps – who can tell you about the sixth peak? They may even know where the Blaggards' camp is.'

Sir Kitry sighed and shook his head. 'I wish it were so, but it seems as though no one in living memory has ever ventured up there. There is a long-held belief among the Pellagaroons that there are strange beings, fiery spirits they call them, that live along the whole of the range. Many people swear that they have seen them dancing from peak to peak on certain nights. No, take my word for it, no one from the Pellagaroo side has been up into the Nine Peaks for a very long time.'

The children looked at each other, both with the same question in mind. Aimi spoke at last. 'What about us? Can we come with you?'

'I do not think so,' said the knight kindly. 'Sir Mons would never allow it. It is far too dangerous. But you are coming with us for part of the way, almost to the foot of the mountains, if that is any consolation. It is a long journey, so the sooner we get started the better. Our transport should be ready and waiting for us.'

'Transport?' asked Dory. 'What transport?'

Sir Kitry rolled his eyes and laughed. 'You shall see. I have a big surprise tucked up my sleeve!' He lifted his arm. 'Or I would have if I had a sleeve to tuck it up!' He began to laugh so infectiously that the children were soon laughing as well, so loudly that none of them realised that Sir Mons was approaching until they heard his voice boom out across the room.

'Come along you three! We have a long way to go. Come along!' His voice was loud, and the children wondered if he was angry, but when Sir Kitry stood with his head bowed and looked down at the ground like a naughty schoolboy, Sir Mons also burst out laughing and slapped him on the back, making a loud 'clang' and causing several heads to peer into the room in alarm.

***

Full of curiosity, Dory and Aimi followed the knights out of the main building and through a stone archway into a stable block where, standing with a young groom, stood two of the biggest horses they had ever seen.

'There,' exclaimed Sir Kitry proudly, 'what do you think of these two beauties?'

Dory stood open-mouthed in amazement. 'Whopper-*oo*!' he gasped, when he had recovered a little. 'What enormous horses!'

'Yes, they are rather large,' agreed Sir Mons. 'They are specially bred to carry a knight in full armour.'

Aimi, too, was astonished at the size of the mounts. 'Do they have names?' she asked.

'Behold Darkuss and Robbin,' Sir Kitry replied, 'fine examples of the equine race and possibly the biggest horses in all of Pellagaroo. Darkuss is the all-black one and the bay with the white markings is Robbin.'

Meanwhile, Sir Mons was opening one of the stable doors. 'And this pretty fellow,' he said, as he led out a sturdy black and white pony, 'is Tamlin.'

Aimi clapped her hands in delight. 'Oh, isn't he lovely! Just like a circus pony.' And then, as the reason for Tamlin being there began to sink in, she looked from one knight to the other and cried, 'Oh, is he for us to ride? Please say that he is. Is he, is he, is he?'

Sir Kitry nodded. 'Yes he is. He really is. He will easily carry both of you and you can take it in turns to hold the reins.'

Aimi turned to Dory and hugged him. 'Can I go at the front first?' she begged. 'Please say you do not mind.' Dory smiled and nodded. It was the first time he had seen her look really happy since they had met.

'You can stay at the front for as long as you like. All the way to...' He looked at Sir Kitry. 'Just where are we going?'

With some difficulty, the knights climbed into their saddles and the children were given a leg-up on to the pony by the groom.

'To Courtly Manor Farm,' replied Sir Kitry, as they all went clattering out of the cobbled yard, 'with a bit of a stop-off on the way.'

From high up on the castle walls came a loud cheer as they trotted away, followed by shouts of 'Good luck!' and 'Long live the Loyals!' And when Dory looked back he saw that a group of knights had gathered there, beneath the golden flags floating so lazily against the sky.

'I wonder if we shall ever see Castle Gardemal again,' he murmured. But Aimi was busy looking ahead, as she proudly held the pony's reins, and seemed not to hear.

***

They rode at an easy pace through the flat countryside, while Sir Kitry told them about the journey ahead.

'Our first stop will be a place we use sometimes when we patrol that far away. It is known as the Old Outpost and does not have much in the way of home comforts, but at least it will give us shelter for the night. We shall travel from there to Courtly Manor Farm. It is the nearest inhabited place to the foot of the mountains. This is where we would like you to stay until we return. We shall leave the horses there. Darkuss and Robbin are much too big and heavy for that sort of journey. It will be narrow in places and very steep.'

'You will love it at the farm,' added Sir Mons. 'It is the home of Squire Uggleton who has a wife and a daughter, Florina. They will look after you well. There are fields where you can play and ride Tamlin, a stream where you can catch fish and many barns and farm animals. They also have two Loyal Protectors to keep them safe. What could be better!'

'Could Tamlin travel up into the mountains?' asked Aimi. 'If so, could we please come with you? We wouldn't hold you up if we could ride him up there. The farm and the squire and his family sound very nice, but I... we would like to come with you to rescue my father.'

Sir Mons shook his head. 'No, it is far too dangerous. Tamlin could get around up there, I am sure, but you will be much safer at the farm.'

'It's for the best,' whispered Dory over Aimi's shoulder. 'We'd only add to their problems. Better to let the knights get on with it in their own way.'

The sun rose up behind them as they progressed, throwing the nodding shadows of the horses across the ground in time with their rocking movement, for mile after mile, until Dory was almost on the point of falling asleep. For a while, they followed the path of a shining river where the horses were allowed to drink. Then their route took them directly across a great tract of grassland where flocks of white birds mingled with more herds of grazing deer. The children ate and drank as they rode, taking food from the saddlebags that hung down on either side of Tamlin's back, and the knights chatted quietly about things that had happened long ago and of adventures that were perhaps yet to come. Yet all eyes were drawn, from time to time, even as they talked, to the huge, craggy mountains that rose up before them, seemingly growing higher and higher with every step that the horses took.

'We should soon be in sight of the Outpost,' said Sir Mons, after what to Dory seemed like hours of riding. 'Let us see who spots it first.'

But it was another twenty minutes or so before the building came into view.

'There,' cried Aimi suddenly, 'is that it, that grey building among those rocks and bushes?'

The knights pulled up their horses and, for a moment, considered the scene in silence.

'Ye-e-s,' replied Sir Kitry, hesitantly. 'That is it.' He turned to Sir Mons.

'I think something is wrong, Captain,' he said quietly. 'What do you make of it?'

Sir Mons stood up in his stirrups to take a better look before answering. He nodded his head. 'You are right,' he said eventually. 'Something is definitely amiss. We need to take a closer look.'

***

As they drew nearer to the building, they saw that some of the roof tiles were missing and that most of the windows were broken. Climbing weeds had begun to cling to the walls and one of the sturdy doors was hanging crookedly open, held by one hinge only.

'Why, it is derelict!' exclaimed Sir Mons. 'It was fine the last time I was out here.'

Inside, they saw that quite a lot of the furniture was damaged. Chairs and tables had been smashed to pieces and broken glass lay all around.

'Someone *has* been busy,' muttered Sir Mons, as he picked up a long piece of dirty fabric and handed one end of it to Sir Kitry, 'and I think I know who.'

He pulled the fabric out to its full length, revealing it to be the tattered remains of the Pellagaroon flag, its golden cloth now covered in mud. Upstairs, the windows were missing some of their panes, and part of the roof was open to the sky, but otherwise the room was relatively undamaged. A table and some chairs were still intact and three bunk beds were seemingly untouched.

A sudden noise made them all spin around. They saw that it was just some owls, blinking down on them from the beams. But it was what was painted on the wall that caught their attention. Crudely drawn in black paint was the outline of a huge bird, its wings outstretched and its cruel beak and talons open as if ready to strike.

'By the Great Zimco!' cried Sir Mons. 'The grizling – the sign of the Blaggards!'

'A pair of those birds attacked us when we first arrived,' said Dory. 'We told Sir Kitry about it. It was only because we ran into a cave that we were able to escape. They very nearly grabbed hold of Aimi. I've never seen such big birds before.'

Aimi shivered as she remembered their ordeal.

'I am not surprised,' said Sir Mons. 'The grizlings are vicious predators, very keen on making off with children and small deer.'

'Vicious predators,' muttered Sir Kitry, 'and a fitting emblem for you know who.'

It was decided that, despite the damage, they would spend the night in what was left of the Old Outpost. The beds were dry and Sir Mons brought in some blankets from his saddlebags while Sir Kitry fetched some lemonade and sandwiches that Mrs Bonny had thoughtfully provided.

'Do not worry about a thing,' said Sir Kitry, as the children climbed into their bunks. 'We do not sleep – the bunks were put in for the occasional human guest – so we shall be here to watch over you. Sir Mons and I will have a game of chess while we chat about old times. Goodnight.'

Chapter 10

It had been a long and tiring day and sleep soon came to them both, but it wasn't long before Dory was awake again and sitting up. Something was wrong. The moonlight was pouring in through the hole in the roof and he was able to see the knights sitting together and hear their quiet murmurings, but something was definitely wrong. He lay back on his bunk and tried to remember his dream – the toast, the breakfast toast! It was burning and his mother was desperately trying to rescue it and fan away the clouds of smoke.

He sat up again, now fully awake, and called to the knights. 'Sir Kitry, Sir Mons! I can smell burning! I think it's coming from downstairs!'

Now there was a loud crackle, followed by a 'whoosh' of flame that shot up past the window from outside, and Dory saw smoke begin to curl up through the floorboards.

'Quick, out of bed, both of you!' shouted Sir Mons. 'Kit, wrap Aimi up in a blanket while I see to Dory. I think we will have to chance the stairway.'

'It is all right,' said Sir Kitry to Aimi, who had just woken up and had not yet grasped what was happening. 'Just trust me and you will be fine.'

Luckily, the stairway was free from fire, but the rest of the downstairs, which was filled with the broken furniture, was now well alight.

'The horses!' cried Sir Mons, once the children were well away from the flames. 'I must see to the horses.' But a few minutes later he was back, leading only Tamlin.

'Darkuss and Robbin have snapped their tethers and run off,' he called. 'Poor Tamlin was not strong enough to break away.'

Aimi ran to Tamlin who was now quivering with fear. 'It's all right, Tamlin,' she soothed, patting his nose and smoothing his coat. 'There, there, you are safe now.' Soon the pony lowered his head and nuzzled her neck as though he understood what she was saying.

'We shall camp out here tonight,' Sir Mons decided, indicating a grassy spot between the trees. 'It is not cold, so if you children just curl up in your blankets you should be quite snug.'

He turned to Sir Kitry. 'What do you think?' he asked. But before Sir Kitry could speak, he answered his own question. 'It *is* them, isn't it?'

Sir Kitry nodded. 'Fires do not start themselves and it is just the sort of cowardly thing they would do.'

Sir Mons walked over to the children, who were both looking uncertain of what to do next.

'Do not worry,' he said, placing his hands on their shoulders. 'We will look after you. Now sleep well and we will see you in the morning.' He turned to Sir Kitry. 'Stay on guard, Kit, while I go and try to find the horses.'

'Will he be all right?' asked Aimi, as the knight strode off into the darkness.

Sir Kitry nodded. 'They would not dare to attack him unless they could catch him unawares. And that,' he added with a chuckle, 'is most unlikely!'

The Old Outpost was now well alight and Dory, rolled up in his blanket, watched as the flames leapt high into the air. From far away he could hear the faint sounds of Sir Mons whistling to the horses and calling their names.

'I do feel safe,' he said to Aimi who lay close by, 'but only when those two are around. They really are Loyal Protectors, aren't they?'

The fire had now reached the top floor of the building and one by one the rafters fell down, making a loud bang and sending tall columns of sparks into the air. He waited for Aimi's reply, but all he could hear was her steady breathing. Higher and higher the sparks climbed into the sky until they reached a point where they seemed to mingle with the stars, so much so that soon he could not tell one from the other and, before long, he too was soundly asleep.

***

Not much was said in the morning as they left the smouldering pile of ashes that was once the Old Outpost. The knights were in sombre mood at the loss of a place full of fond memories, but as the day became brighter, so, it seemed, did they. They began to chat and even laughed and shook their heads ruefully at the thought that no one had ever been clever enough to equip the knights with a sense of smell, so what a good thing it was that Dory had woken up when he did. Sir Kitry even began to sing for a while in a language that none of the others could understand.

'Is that the ancient dialect?' asked Sir Mons. 'I did not know that you could speak it.'

Sir Kitry held up his hand. 'No, no,' he said modestly, 'I cannot – only that song. Doctor Hugo taught it to me.' He laughed. 'Had it wired into me, in fact, so that at least a little of the language would remain before it died out completely. The song tells of the life of the Gargants, a race of giants who supposedly inhabited this land before it became known as Pellagaroo. All very romantic stuff, but none the worse for that.'

All through the morning they rode, mostly in single file, through the ever-changing countryside, sometimes through grasses that were so tall that they came up to the children's waists, making little Tamlin almost disappear from sight, and sometimes over ground that was red and sandy, where strange trees with long, thick trunks and huge leaves grew in groups of three and four.

'They look like big sticks of rhubarb,' commented Dory.

Aimi smiled at the thought. 'They do. I wonder if the giants who lived here ever had rhubarb tart for tea?'

'With buckets of custard,' laughed Dory. 'All served in a bowl the size of a bathtub!'

Suddenly, Sir Mons, who was in the lead, stopped and held up his hand. 'A pair of grizlings ahead!' he shouted. 'Coming up over that clump of trees to our right. Watch out for the children, Kit!'

Sir Kitry turned to Dory and Aimi. 'Do not worry, Sir Mons will deal with them!'

But the birds flew high over their heads without attempting to attack them and it was only when Aimi happened to look over her shoulder, and the others heard her scream of terror, that the knights realised they had been tricked. The birds had turned and were attacking from the rear! They were now swooping down towards the children, as Sir Kitry swivelled round in the saddle just in time to release a stream of firepower at the leading bird. The grizling immediately came out of its dive and rose into the air, causing the strike to miss its body, but catching it in the tail and setting its feathers on fire. It was not a fatal hit, but it was enough. The second bird then veered away, leaving its mate to flap slowly back up into the sky with burning tail feathers spiralling down to the ground.

'Good shooting!' cried Sir Mons. 'But they nearly caught us by surprise.'

After the children had recovered a little from their ordeal, the knights reassured them as much as they could that the birds were very unlikely to launch another attack, but explained that, just to be on the safe side, they would ride the rest of the way three abreast with Tamlin and the children in the middle. Nevertheless, it was a very relieved Dory and Aimi who heard Sir Mons declare that they were very near to their journey's end.

'There it is,' he cried at last, shielding his eyes from the sunlight. 'Courtly Manor Farm. Just four firepower lengths away.' Ahead, the children saw a long farmhouse surrounded by crop-filled fields and orchards full of fruit.

'All seems well,' said Sir Kitry. 'Smoke in the chimney and washing on the line.'

'And Loyal Protectors at home,' added Sir Mons, pointing at the flag flying above the house.

They were met at the farmyard gate by a young woman waving a bright yellow duster in welcome. 'We've been looking out for you for ages,' she said. 'Our dear Loyal Sir Renade met one of your knights earlier on patrol who told him you were coming. And now here you are! All safe and sound. Welcome, Sir Mons, Sir Kitry. It's been such a long time since we've seen you!'

She turned to the children. 'Now let me see if I've got this right. You must be Dory and you must be Aimi. What pretty names! Just you both come along with Florina – that's me,' she said, giving a little bow. 'Now don't fret about your pony, Miss Aimi. Our man Tod will see to him and his two big brothers as well.'

'We shall see you later,' said Sir Kitry to Dory and Aimi. 'Go along with Florina and she will look after you. We are going to have a chat with the squire – a few things to sort out. Nothing for you to worry about.'

Florina led them into a big kitchen where they were met by the delicious smell of baked pastry.

'Our visitors have arrived, mother,' she said to a grey-haired, kindly-looking woman who was setting out plates on the table. 'As hungry as birds in the snow, aren't you my pets?'

Mrs Uggleton beamed. 'You've come to the right place, my dears. I was just wondering what to do with this big meat pie, all fresh from the oven!'

'And don't forget the gooseberry tart,' added Florina. 'Mustn't let that go to waste.'

The kitchen was warmed by a big iron stove and the rays from its hot coals flowed into the room, making the copper pots and pans twinkle and the blue and white plates on the dresser shine. As the children sat at the table while Mrs Uggleton and Florina bustled around them, piling their plates high with food, they smiled and nodded to one another as they shared their sudden relief. Courtly Manor Farm was the very next best thing to home and with these kind people they would be really safe and would both sleep very well tonight.

***

When the dishes had been cleared away and Mrs Uggleton had left to attend to other matters, Florina and the children sat by the fire and chatted quietly together.

'Tell me about the Other Side,' said Florina. 'I mean, the place where you come from. Is it anything like Pellagaroo?'

Dory thought for a moment. 'It is in some ways,' he said. 'We have fields and farms and horses and other animals, but we also have cars and trains and aeroplanes which I don't think you do. So perhaps Pellagaroo is something like our home was a long time ago.'

Florina shook her head. 'No, we don't have those things, whatever they are, but we do have our own dear Loyals. Do you have those?'

The children laughed. 'No,' said Aimi, 'we don't, but it would be nice if we did. I wish Sir Kitry and Sir Mons would come home with us.'

'We had knights once upon a time,' added Dory. 'There was a king, King Arthur, who had a band of knights who all sat together at a round table, and *they* were very loyal.'

There was the sound of laughter in the yard outside. Dory went to the window where he saw Sirs Kitry and Mons talking to two new arrivals.

Florina told them, 'They're our Loyals, Sir Renade and Sir Kuss. Those four are old friends. They'll be sharing quarters tonight in the rooms across the yard. I expect Sirs Kitry and Mons will be off to an early start tomorrow.'

Aimi joined them at the window. 'I wish I was going with them, but Sir Mons says it is too dangerous for us up there.'

Florina looked shocked. 'Dangerous!' she cried. 'Did you say *dangerous*? I can't believe you'd want to go anywhere near that place. You wouldn't get me to go there at any price. The peaks are haunted and sometimes the whole range shines with a ghostly light – green as a lump of mouldy cheese it is, and worse than that, it's home to the fiery spirits. Many a night I've seen them dancing about up there.' She shuddered. 'Nightmares I've had because of them. And it's not just me who's seen them. My old granny saw them too, and her mother before her.'

She crouched forward until she was close to their faces, and sang in a voice that was almost a whisper:

Up in the mountains of Pellagaroo,
The spirits are dancing
And calling to you.

You'll join in their antics
'Til you're out of breath,
Unable to stop
'Til you dance to your death!

'That's what my gran used to sing to me,' she said.
'Just you think yourself lucky, child, that you're to stay down here with Florina Uggleton and leave the spookery-dookery to those knights. They're not frightened of anything.

Chapter 11

When Dory woke up the following day, he found himself in a bright and cheerful bedroom with quaint old furniture and diamond-paned windows that the sun was busy turning into dozens of tiny rainbows. He had been too tired to take much notice of his surroundings the night before when Florina had shown them where they were to sleep.

'Here we are,' she had said. 'Two cosy rooms right next door to each other, so that you won't feel too lonely.' And now he smiled as he opened his eyes and saw the patchwork quilt that was so similar to the one on his bed at home.

He looked out of the window and clearly saw, for the first time, the great size of the mountain range that lay directly ahead. One, two, three... he counted until he came to the sixth peak – the one by which the knights were hoping to gain entry. The other eight peaks presented a solid wall of rock, menacing and sheer with no sign of even one foothold, but on peak six he could just make out a track, which appeared and disappeared at intervals as it travelled upwards, before eventually vanishing from view.

The knights obviously had a hard journey ahead of them, but, like Aimi, he rather wished he was going with them. He washed and dressed as quickly as he could and hurried down the stairs. If he couldn't go with them, at least he could say goodbye and wish them a safe journey. But when he reached the bottom he was met by a very downcast Aimi.

'They have gone!' she said sadly. 'The knights have left without saying goodbye. I got up really early, but they must have left at first light. Sir Kuss has ridden with them to the foot of the mountains so that he can bring Darkuss and Robbin back to the farm. Oh, Dory, I wanted to warn them, to tell them to be careful. I know there is trouble ahead.'

Dory looked at her face and was alarmed by what he saw. There was real fear in her bright eyes, as though she actually *knew* that something bad was going to happen.

'Trouble?' he asked. 'What sort of trouble?'

Aimi put her finger to her lips and beckoned him to follow her upstairs. 'Please don't think I am being silly,' she said when they reached the bedroom, 'but last night I had a very bad dream. The knights were in difficulty – I do not know how or where exactly – but it was somewhere dark and horrible. It was all so real that I felt I was there with them, trapped, where their firepower could not save them and even Sir Mons was helpless. I wanted to tell them about it, but now it is too late!'

Dory went to the window and together they stared at the great mass of stone that marked the boundary between Pellagaroo and whatever land was hidden on the other side.

'Look!' cried Aimi, grabbing his arm suddenly and pointing ahead. 'Look, look there!'

He peered against the light, following the direction of her outstretched arm, until he managed to focus on what had caused her such alarm. There, circling slowly over the sixth peak, were half a dozen black specks, far, far away, but unmistakable.

'Grizlings,' he said quietly. 'Horrible grizlings!'

Aimi gripped his arm tightly and he guessed that she was remembering their previous encounters with the fearsome creatures.

'We'd better go down,' he said after a while. 'I expect breakfast will soon be ready. Perhaps it's best we say nothing about your dream, at least not yet.'

Aimi nodded and smiled, but there was still a look of fear in her eyes that filled him with unease. Perhaps her dream really was a warning of some kind and the knights were heading into danger.

***

They saw Squire Uggleton for the first time as they sat down to breakfast. He was a jolly, red-faced man with a mop of white hair who sat at the head of the table and waved and encouraged them to 'eat up' from time to time, as he lifted an empty spoon to his mouth and pretended to chew an imaginary mouthful of food.

After they had eaten, he introduced himself by saying 'Squire Uggleton welcomes you to Courtly Manor' and asked them what they would like to do for the rest of the day.

'You can have a look around the farm,' he told them. 'I'm rather busy, but Tod will be happy to show you; or take a picnic down by the stream; or ride your pony, but don't go too far – always stay in sight of the farm and you will be safe. Sir Renade will be on patrol this morning, and later Sir Kuss will take over when he gets back with the horses.'

It was decided that they would look around the farm and they found Tod, the young man who had taken care of Tamlin when they had arrived, more than happy to act as their guide.

'This is better than cleaning out the stables,' he said, with a smile and a wink, 'but then again', taking off his cap and scratching his head, 'I'll still have to do 'em sometime, won't I? Come along then, there's someone you'll be wanting to see, I'm sure.'

He led the way to a large paddock and there, grazing with some of the other horses, and looking rather small in their company, was Tamlin.

'Tamlin, Tamlin!' cried Aimi, as she climbed on to the paddock fence and waved her arms. 'Over here, boy, over here!'

There was a joyful reunion as Aimi hugged the pony's neck and stroked his nose, while the other horses looked loftily on as if to say, 'What's all the fuss about?' Then, as Dory and Tod started to move off, she whispered, 'I'll see you later and I'll bring you a nice big apple.'

Next, they visited the 'squealers', as Tod called the young pigs, then the lambs, where Aimi fed some of the younger ones from a bottle, and the duck pond, and the milking shed – and for a while the gloom that had hung over them lifted a little as they became absorbed with the daily goings-on of farm life. But, when Tod had returned to his duties and they were walking back to the house, they felt again the brooding presence of the mountains hanging over them, and they were both having the same thought: how were the knights faring up there? Were they protected by their firepower, or was it possible that they were in danger and in need of help?

***

'I want to go after them,' said Aimi quickly, as they neared the farmhouse. Jup, one of the farm dogs, came barking up the path as she spoke, and Dory thought that he had misheard what she had said. There was a garden seat under one of the apple trees nearby. So he sat down, quietened the dog and looked up at her.

'I mean it,' she went on. 'I have been thinking about it all morning.' She sat beside him and, before he could say anything, continued, 'We could go on Tamlin. You know how strong he is – for a pony, I mean – and Sir Mons said that a smaller horse would be able to travel up there. You heard him yourself. Dory, I want to go. I have this awful feeling that I should. The knights have been so kind and protective, I feel we owe it to them. Also, if they are in a fix of some sort, how will I ever find my father? What do you think? Will you come with me?'

Dory shook his head. 'Go up there?' he cried, glancing up at the mountains. 'On our own? With grizlings and Blaggards and fiery wotsits and goodness knows what else lurking about! It's not possible. It's crazy! And anyway,' he added, nodding in the direction of the house, 'they would never let us.'

But Aimi persisted. 'I have been thinking about that,' she said quickly. 'We could go when the knights change patrols. They are bound to spend a little time together before one of them takes over. We could say we were going for a ride on Tamlin, take a picnic down by the stream, and then, when the time is right, make a run for it.'

Dory looked at the Nine Peaks. 'Just look at it! Look at the size of it all. How would we even know where to start? And if we did go, it'd probably be a wild goose chase. I mean, a dream – it's not much to go on, is it?'

Aimi pointed at the sixth peak, which lay almost directly in line with the farmhouse. 'There, that's where the trail starts. One way up and one way down. All we would have to do is to stay on the track.'

Dory shook his head again. 'It's still only a dream that's making you act like this. And if we did go, it would be a bit of a dirty trick, wouldn't it, running off after all they've done for us, showing us nothing but kindness?'

He looked at her for a reply, but she said nothing. He noticed how calm she seemed and, not for the first time, thought how brave she could be when she had made her mind up about something.

'Aimi,' he said, 'did you hear me – nothing but kindness?'

She nodded, but said nothing. And when she did eventually speak, she had a faraway look in her eyes.

'When I was at home in Japan,' she began, 'I had a cousin. He was a little older than me and we often played together. He was a very adventurous boy, always going off on his own and getting into scrapes of one kind or another. One day he went out to play and did not come home. That night, while his father and some of the neighbours went out to search for him, I had a very strange dream. I saw a tall white tower on a high cliff, and I heard a roaring noise like the sea makes when the waves are driven up in a storm, and I heard a voice calling for help. It was awful because I could not help, and the voice kept calling and calling until I woke up in a great fright, and I did not know why.' She paused, and Dory saw how pale she suddenly appeared as she relived the moments of the dream. He said nothing because he knew that she had more to say.

'The next morning,' she continued, 'when the search party returned without my cousin, I told his father about my dream and some of the men overheard what I said and laughed. But one of them said, "I know that tower. It is a sort of watchtower or lighthouse. I went there myself when I was a boy – it was a bit of a ruin even then, but it could still be there." Well, they went out again, even though they had been searching all night, and when they reached the tower they found my cousin inside on the floor with his leg broken. He had been climbing up the staircase and it had given way.'

'And was he all right,' asked Dory, 'apart from the broken leg, I mean?

Aimi smiled and nodded vigorously. 'His leg was rather crooked, and he walked with a limp, but otherwise he was fine.'

'And what about you? Were you praised for what you did? Given a medal, or something?

'Of course not. I did nothing brave.' She frowned as though she was trying to recall something else that had happened. 'But later,' she said eventually, 'one of the older men said that I must be blessed with... well, the nearest thing in English is "second sight", but that is not a very good example. It is something that some children have – the ability to warn of danger – and they only keep it for a short time, gradually losing it as they grow older.'

***

Dory looked at the farmhouse with its nut-brown, thatched roof and its tall chimneys. In the garden, Florina was gathering peas for the mid-day meal. Everything looked so peaceful, yet danger was never very far away.

'Now I'm *really* stumped,' he said. 'And I don't quite know what to do. If we did go, run off like that, what about them, the Uggletons? They'd be worried to pieces, and wouldn't they think that we'd betrayed them?'

Aimi agreed. 'Yes, of course – at first, anyway. But I think, in time, they would forgive us. We could leave them a note where they would be sure to find it after we had gone. We could tell them how sorry we are but that we feel that Sir Kitry and Sir Mons are in danger. Dory, I am sure that the knights are heading into some kind of trouble – or may be in it already. I think we should go and try to find them.'

Florina had now finished her pea-picking and she turned and waved at them before going back into the house. It was a sad moment, and Dory felt a rush of guilt as he raised his hand in reply. He made one last attempt to change Aimi's mind.

'How would it be if we told Sir Renade and Sir Kuss everything,' he asked, 'and let them deal with it? I'm sure they wouldn't hesitate to go to the rescue if they thought other Loyals were in danger.'

But Aimi had thought of that and shook her head. 'Remember what Sir Kitry said about the big horses being unable to travel up there? Sir Renade and Sir Kuss would have to go on foot, and I do not think they would leave Courtly Manor unprotected for very long just because a little girl had a nightmare. Also, they know that both Sir Kitry and Sir Mons are equipped with firepower. What could possibly happen to them?'

Dory looked up at the sixth peak. They called it the 'Dog's Nose,' but his imaginative mind now saw the head of a wolf that was about to howl at the sky. A flutter of anxiety crept into his stomach, but somehow he forced himself to smile.

'You're right,' he said, 'you're always right! We'd better make a plan.'

Chapter 12

'Can we ride Tamlin after we have eaten?' asked Aimi, as she helped Florina to lay the table.

'Better ask Ma. She's in the kitchen – it's baking day. I'm sure she'll say yes.'

Mrs Uggleton, rolling pin in hand, looked up as Aimi approached. 'Of course you can, my dear,' she said when Aimi repeated the question. 'But don't stray too far. There's a pretty little spot in the lower meadow, under a crop of willows right next to the stream. Tell you what, I'll make you up a picnic – some boiled egg sandwiches, some lemonade and a couple of these custard tarts I've just baked. Goodness, you won't want any tea after that, will you?' She placed a floury imprint on Aimi's nose and added, 'Which is a pity, because I'm making a big strawberry flan, topped with cream, and you'll just have to go without! Now go and ask Tod to get the pony ready for after lunch.'

She gave Aimi a hug, which left more flour on her face, and then looked into her eyes. 'And mind what I said about not straying too far from the farm.'

'What have you been up to?' asked Dory, when they met at the top of the stairs. 'You're covered in white powder.'

Aimi looked down at her feet. 'It was awful,' she said, as she told him about what had happened in the kitchen. 'She is so kind, and I feel rather ashamed of myself.'

Dory produced a small piece of paper. 'Don't let's talk about it anymore. I've written this note, saying how grateful we are for their kindness explaining why we're going and saying how sorry we are. You're doing what you think is the right thing. I just hope they realise that.'

***

'We'd better make sure we don't meet up with Sir Kuss,' said Dory, as they jogged off astride Tamlin, 'or we can say goodbye to our trip, for sure. We'll go down to the stream. We can watch the farm from there. As soon as we see him ride in with the horses, we'll head for the foot of the mountain.'

It was, as Mrs Uggleton had suggested, a pretty spot for a picnic. The water sparkled in the sunlight, and colourful dragonflies and kingfishers flitted about above the stream, while minnows lay in little groups under the trailing branches of the willow trees. Yet, despite their surroundings, neither of them felt relaxed enough to unpack the food, nor even to sit beside the stream. They just stood, silent and filled with thoughts of the task they were about to undertake, as Tamlin pulled on the sweet grass nearby before wandering down to drink his fill at the water's edge.

'I hope we haven't missed him – Sir Kuss,' said Dory after a while. 'I've been looking out for him.'

But Aimi assured him that she, too, had not taken her eyes off the farm entrance. 'I am sure he will be along soon,' she said, and when he eventually arrived they saw that they needn't have been concerned. The spectacle of the knight with the blue and gold banner held aloft on his lance, the thudding sound of the three heavy horses as they galloped towards the farm, kicking up lumps of turf as they went, and Sir Kuss's hearty cry of 'Halloo the farm' would have been unlikely to have passed unnoticed.

'We had better go further downstream,' said Aimi, as they climbed on to Tamlin's back. 'If we do that, we are less likely to be spotted when we make a dash for the mountains.'

But they *were* spotted. As soon as they left the stream and had begun to race across the open stretch of meadow, they heard a loud barking sound and saw to their dismay that the dog, Jup, was hurtling towards them.

'Go home, Jup,' they both shouted. 'Go home, boy!'

But Jup continued to run after them, barking wildly, as if this was all a game, and one that he was determined not to be left out of.

Aimi clung on to Dory's waist as tightly as she could, hoping with all her heart that she would not fall off, and fully expecting to hear the sounds of pursuit from the knights at the farm. It was an anxious mile or two before Jup gave up the chase and she was able to report that, surprisingly, they were not being followed.

'Mustn't tire you out, must we, boy,' said Dory, as he reined the pony in and they continued at an easy jog. 'We might have quite a climb ahead of us.'

But Tamlin was far from tired. He seemed to have enjoyed the high-speed run they had made, and nodded his head and pranced in a high-spirited way as they approached the start of the mountain track.

The climb was not steep at first, little more than a slight incline, and the way was well-defined between walls of rock with no way of straying off course. Flowers grew here and there between boulders and smaller stones and ferns pushed out from cracks in the rock face, brushing the children's heads as they passed by and splashing them with dew from out of the dark shadows. But the strangest thing was the moss which seemed to cling to every available flat surface, thick as a carpet. Curling and moist and a most unusual shade of green, it gave the impression that the whole mountain was covered with fur.

'A fur coat for a mountain,' said Aimi, 'to keep it warm, maybe!' She shivered as she spoke, as the temperature had gradually dropped as they travelled higher and where the sides of the trail blocked out the last of the sun's rays.

Soon, the way became steeper, so much so that Tamlin's hooves began to slip against the hard surface of the trail and both the children had to dismount and continue on foot. Up and up they climbed, sometimes riding and sometimes not, often losing sight of much of the sky as the stone walls towered above them. It was a great relief to them both when the track began to curl back towards the Pellagaroon side of the mountain and they found themselves in the open once more.

'Tamlin is hungry,' Aimi pointed out, as the pony dropped his head and made his way to some clumps of grass growing nearby. 'And so am I,' she added. 'Shall we give him a rest and eat the picnic food?'

Dory climbed on to a ledge of rock and looked back at the place they had left behind them. His eye swept over the grass-covered plain, the stream wandering between the trees, the farmhouse, tiny now beside its lengthening shadows, and, beyond that, the Great Thicket – the tangled woodland where they had fled in terror from the Bellman before finding Sir Kitry. Further still, he saw the edge of the land, perhaps the very spot at which they had arrived, curved like a horseshoe within the seemingly lifeless sea which stretched away to a horizon of nothingness. Was that where his home lay, he wondered, or was it just close by, as Sir Kitry had said?

'The way ahead will soon turn inwards again,' he said, 'probably right across to the other side of the mountain. So if you want to take a last look at Pellagaroo you'd better do it now.' He stretched out a hand and pulled Aimi up beside him and together they looked out over the landscape.

'They must have missed us by now,' she said, 'and be ever so worried.'

Dory nodded, and in his mind he saw a picture of Florina's face peering anxiously out of the window, hoping in vain to catch a glimpse of the two runaways.

There was smoke rising up from one of the chimneys, a thin spiral of blue, and he remembered how safe and comfortable he had felt as soon as they had entered the farm and how kind the Uggleton family had been to them. Aimi and he had left all that behind and were now halfway up a mountain in a strange land with no idea of what lay in store for them. They had no protection and no means of getting home and now, stronger than ever before, a feeling of despair came over him. What was he to do? He looked at Aimi and saw that she had been watching his face, but before he could say anything she shook her head.

'No,' she said, as if she had been reading his thoughts. 'Not now, not when we have come this far. We have to go on. I know how you feel, but we have to believe that everything will turn out well in the end. If we go back, it will all have been for nothing.'

They sat on the ledge and ate the picnic food in silence, Dory again feeling very aware of Aimi's ability to behave in a very grown-up way when the occasion required it. She put her hand into one of the paper bags and smiled.

'Hey, presto!' she exclaimed, as she pulled out an apple as though she was a conjuror. 'Some little pony is going to be very lucky indeed.'

***

The track ahead did indeed turn inwards and they were once again enclosed on either side by the mountain walls.

'Remember what Sir Kitry said about giants once living in Pellagaroo?' asked Aimi, after a while. 'Well, I think it must have been giants who cut these passages through the rock. They cannot be a natural part of the mountain, can they?'

Dory, his gloomy thoughts having now been put aside, laughed. 'It sounds a bit far-fetched. Florina told us that there were fiery spirits hopping about up here, but I haven't seen any sign of them yet!'

Aimi looked up at the sky. 'Nor grizlings. Let's hope it stays that way!'

At last, the trail levelled out and they saw that it was unlikely to climb any higher. The summit of the sixth peak still rose above them and they were now in a position to view the other eight. Five stretched away on one side of them and three on the other, all looking like tall, hooded figures cloaked by shadows as the light began to fade, and some with thin, white clouds continually rolling, breaking up and then reforming at their feet.

Dusk began to settle, and as it did so a soft green light, no more than a glimmering at first, began to spread across the ground, making Tamlin come to an abrupt halt and causing the children to look around in alarm. As the sky darkened, so the light seemed to grow stronger, and it began to run in little ripples up and down the sides of the mountains, making each of the peaks pulsate with a mysterious and ghostly glow. Large rocks were piled high on either side of the track and tall weeds grew among them in profusion. These, too, were bathed in the same peculiar shade of green.

'There's no way to escape it,' said Dory. 'I don't like it, but perhaps it won't harm us. We'd better press on. At least we'll be able to see where we're going.'

But Tamlin seemed reluctant to move, and when they did finally manage to coax him forwards, he did so slowly, picking his legs up high with every step and making odd snuffling sounds.

'Poor Tamlin,' sighed Aimi. 'He is usually so obedient. He is acting as if he is terrified. If only we could get him away from this weird green stuff. I am sure that is what is worrying him.'

They walked beside the pony, talking to him quietly, but now and then he stopped and his ears twitched as though he was listening to something. Then he became seemingly stuck to the ground in terror and would not move, however hard Aimi tugged at his bridle.

'He can hear something,' said Dory, as the pony's ears moved frantically backwards and forwards and his eyes rolled around in fright. 'It's not just the green stuff. He can hear something – and so can I!'

Now Aimi could hear it too, a drumming sound that clicked and clattered around the mountain walls, as the ground began to vibrate under their feet. Their immediate instinct was to run, but which way? Then, looking back, they saw a group of dancing lights that seemed to be getting bigger, darting from side to side and gradually taking the shape of leaping figures, each covered in flames that flickered and shone through the semi-darkness. And Tamlin still seemed unable to move, no matter how hard they pushed and tugged him.

'Get up on his back,' said Dory, 'while I pull on his bridle. Dig your heels in hard and shout his name. We've got to get away from here right now!'

He gave her a leg up into the saddle and tugged the bridle as hard as he could, until at last Tamlin began to move, slowly at first, and then breaking into a canter, so that Dory suddenly found it difficult to keep up.

'Hurry up!' shouted Aimi, as he began to lag behind. 'I think they are gaining on us!' And then, almost in the same breath, as she pulled the pony to a skidding halt, 'A cave! There on the left. Let us go in there. Hurry up!'

***

The cave, which was big enough to admit Tamlin as well, had appeared at just the right time. As soon as they had managed to scramble through the entrance, it was lit by a series of flashes and filled with a roar of sound which echoed around its walls for the few moments it took the strange creatures to pass by.

'The... fiery... spirits,' panted Aimi, as they sat in the welcome silence that followed. 'Florina... was... right... after... all.'

Dory nodded. 'Thank goodness you spotted this cave when you did,' he said, when at last he was able to speak. 'Those things, those fiery things, were almost upon us. I've never been so scared. I really thought my heart was going to burst. And Tamlin was terrified as well.'

They sat on the floor of the cave for a while. Then Aimi went to the entrance and peered cautiously out. 'No sign of them now. Looks like we have found somewhere for the night, unless there are any more surprises in store for us.'

Dory crept to the back of the cave, where he thought they might feel a bit safer, but he was soon back with worrying news. He put his finger to his lips. 'I don't like it,' he said quietly. 'This cave is the entrance to a tunnel. It curves away, and there's a light – a flickering light – coming from up there. Let's get out of here right now!'

But, as he took hold of Tamlin's bridle, they heard a voice echoing down to them.

'Do not go. Please come in. Do not be afraid. Bring the little horse in with you. There is plenty of room. You can find sanctuary here.'

'What do you think?' whispered Dory when he had recovered a little from his surprise. 'Shall we chance it? At least it sounds as if there's a human being up there and not one of those... *things!*'

Aimi nodded. 'I *am* very tired, and this seems a better idea than going back out into the darkness. Let us go in and hope for the best.'

Chapter 13

The light sent their shadows dancing and looming above their heads and across the walls, making the situation they were in seem even scarier, and it was a great relief when they found, at last, the cause of it. Peering around the corner, they saw that the tunnel had now opened up into a large chamber, in the centre of which a fire was burning, sending up bright flames and long columns of smoke that disappeared through a hole in the ceiling.

'Of course,' the voice went on, 'you are very cautious, and rightly so. Perhaps, like many others who have travelled here before you, you have made a long and tiring journey, which has not been without its problems, but have no fear – you shall come to no harm in the place where you now find yourselves.'

Stepping into the room, they saw that it was quite square and had obviously been carved out of the rock. The walls were smooth and many recesses had been provided for stone jars, colourful glass bottles and various small pots and boxes. There were hooks in the ceiling and, from these, hung bundles of dried flowers, long, seed-filled grasses and bunches of herbs. They filled the room with sweet smells and faded colours of every hue as they swayed from time to time in the currents of warm air. The children looked around for the person who had invited them in, but there was no one to be seen.

'That's a bit odd,' whispered Dory, 'but I've a feeling that we're being watched.'

Then they heard the voice again, as a little brown-faced man appeared from behind them, so quickly that they both stepped back in surprise.

'My name is Ranjee,' said the little man in a pleasant, musical voice, nodding his head up and down as he spoke. 'Welcome to my home. Please sit at my table. You must be hungry and thirsty. Come, come, honoured guests.'

There were several iron pots simmering at the fireside, and from one of these Ranjee filled two bowls with what looked like thick porridge.

'My own special mixture of nuts and gruel,' he said as he set the bowls down in front of them. 'Just as I used to eat in the Old Country – and look, here is honey from the wild bees. I think you will find it very delicious.'

Delicious it was, and they were both so hungry that they didn't realise that Ranjee had left them until he came bustling back into the room carrying a pail of water and a bundle of hay for Tamlin.

'Your little horse is suffering from fright,' he said, 'so I would like, if you please, to give him some herbs that will help to make him calm once more.'

He stroked the pony's nose and began to talk to him in a foreign language, nodding his head again as he did so and feeding Tamlin the herbs by hand. Soon the pony was nodding his head as if in reply.

When they had eaten, the children sat with Ranjee beside the fire and sipped the sweet herbal drink that he had made for them, telling him of their recent frightful experience. But when they came to mention the 'fiery spirits,' he began to laugh.

'Hee, hee, hee,' he cried, 'ho, ho, ho! Yes, oh my goodness, yes, the fiery spirits – those most dangerous of creatures!' Then, seeing the puzzled looks on the children's faces, he said, 'Oh, please forgive me. How very impolite of me. You have had a very bad time. What am I thinking of to behave in such an unseemly manner!'

For a moment or two he was very quiet, as if he was afraid he might start laughing again, but when he had fully regained his composure he said, 'Please come with me. I have something I wish to show you. Do not be alarmed at what you are about to see. I am with you, so you are quite safe.'

***

They followed him through an opening at the back of the chamber. Despite his words of reassurance, what they saw made them shrink back in fear, and it was only Ranjee's hands on their shoulders and his calm voice that prevented them from running away. There in the darkness stood a creature that seemed to be on fire. Every part of its body shone with light, and its yellow eyes gleamed out at them with a terrifying stare. Ranjee steered them back into the main chamber and took down a bright lantern that was hanging nearby.

'Now let us take another look,' he said. They followed him back through the opening, and by the lantern's light saw that they were in a long, narrow room where there were several cages, most of which contained birds and other animals.

'My patients,' said Ranjee, spreading his arms wide, 'and this room is my hospital.'

At the sound of his voice, a great screeching and squawking started up, as the creatures jumped and ran around, each clamouring for his attention.

'There, there,' he said soothingly, as he fed each of them with nuts and seeds and other titbits from his pockets. 'You will all soon be well enough to go out into the fresh air again.'

He turned to the children. 'These mountains can be a very dangerous place, and Doctor Ranjee always has a houseful of guests needing attention – a broken wing, perhaps, or a joint out of place, a baby bird that has been abandoned, or even a broken bone. All of these need looking after.'

He led them to where a goat with its leg in plaster, and looking rather sorry for itself, was tethered. 'Yes, a very dangerous place indeed.'

He went round the cages again, nodding to every occupant as he passed them: the crow, the squirrel, the great owl, the sparrow and the little fox, and each one fell silent and still as he did so.

'How do you manage to control them?' asked Aimi. 'These animals are usually so wild.'

Ranjee smiled and placed a gentle hand on her shoulder. 'Control is not the right word. The word is "love" – always love.'

They returned to the main chamber and sat by the fire, and Aimi asked a question for them both. 'But what happened to the creature that was on fire? Where did it go?'

Ranjee laughed. 'It was the *goat*! That is all it was – the goat with the broken leg. It was just the goat. I will show you.'

He went to one of the recesses in the wall and came back with a pinch of green, springy material to which he then added a tiny drop of water.

'Behold! Ranjee the magician!' He cupped it in his hands. To their amazement, a light now began to shine out from between his fingers.

'This is candlemoss,' he said. 'You must have seen it on your way up here. It grows everywhere, especially on the rock face. It is a kind of moss that shines in the dark when it gets damp. That is why the whole mountain sometimes gives off such an eerie light. The dew, or even a slight mist, is often enough to start it glowing.'

The thought of it made him laugh again, and in between giggles he continued, 'The goats eat it and when it gets dark their hairy coats light up. So as they leap across the mountain tops, as goats do – hocus pocus! – fiery spirits are seen by the good folk down below. I should not laugh, I know, but it is all so very comical!'

'Candlemoss!' exclaimed Dory. 'What fantastic stuff! The glowing mountain, the fiery spirits, all caused by an old plant. Whatever would Florina say if she knew?'

Ranjee pointed to the lanterns that were hung around the walls. 'An old plant, yes, but a most useful old plant. See how brightly the light shines down upon us. The Ancients taught me how to use it when I was newly arrived in this strange place. They also instructed me in the various uses of the other plants found here.' He waved his hand around the room. 'See all the potions and ointments I have. There are plants for ills of all kinds, and Ranjee has samples of every one of them.'

Suddenly, he started to walk around the room selecting ferns, flowers and herbs from those that hung from the ceiling. He brought them to the fireside and said, 'Tonight I must read the smoke again. Hopefully I shall see something there that will be of help to you.'

'Read the smoke?' asked Dory. 'What do you mean? And who are the Ancients?'

Ranjee poured them out some more of the herbal drink, then sat down beside the fire with them.

***

'The Ancient Ones – those wise and gentle people. Alas, I think they must now all be gone, although there may be one or two of their descendants here and there. I was one of the earlier newcomers to arrive here. They made me welcome. I think they believed that I was one of them. I certainly could have passed for a relation of theirs in looks. Their race was dying out, even then, and I suppose they wanted someone they felt they could trust to pass their secrets on to. To be taught to read the smoke was useful too. That is why I wasn't surprised when you arrived. I saw you... well, not *you* exactly, but the vision of "two small riders on a little horse", as the smoke foretold it last night, long before you came rushing into my entrance-way. There was also something about a quest for somebody or something, but then the smoke died away and the rest of the message never came.'

Dory began to explain why they were there. 'We're looking for...', but Ranjee cut him short before he could finish.

'Say nothing more, if you please. The smoke is like that. It never gives the full picture, but leaves it open, so that the reader can use his or her own instinctive power to complete the story in the right way. I must not be influenced by any more information. You are on a quest, that is all I need to know. Tonight, when you are asleep, I shall see what more it has to reveal.'

He pointed at the far end of the room. 'There are beds ready for you when you wish to sleep. Blankets on top of layers of soft mountain grasses, which I hope you will find most comfortable.'

'How did you get here,' asked Aimi. 'Did you discover an entrance, like we did?

Ranjee nodded. 'Well, yes, I suppose I did in a way, but not by choice. Unlike you both, who came here with a brave purpose, I was an accidental traveller. One day, as I was sitting among the mountain peaks of my homeland, seeking enlightenment as I so often did, I slipped and, almost before I knew what was happening, I fell through the air. Down and down I went, fully expecting to die on the stony floor of the valley, but instead I felt a kind of force. A great strength suddenly took hold of me, and the next thing I knew was that I was standing on my feet in this country, close to the dormant sea that touches its shores, and I have been here ever since.' He sighed and shook his head. 'That was almost one hundred years ago.' he added. 'Where has the time gone?'

The children looked with disbelief at his bright brown eyes, his strong white teeth and the dark hair that hung down to his shoulders.

'Do you mean to say that you're over one hundred years old?' asked Dory. 'I can hardly believe it!'

Ranjee closed his eyes and began to nod his head, moving his lips as he did so, as if he was perhaps counting the years that had passed.

'Ranjee is one hundred and twenty-one years old, and that is the truth.'

***

There was a blue flower among the plants that Ranjee had laid by the fire, and Aimi picked it up and raised it to her nose.

'That should not be there,' said Ranjee. 'It must have got mixed in with the tiddle-worts by mistake. It has no scent and is of no medicinal use, but it is quite beautiful, is it not? You must have seen it on your travels. It covers the land as if it were a reflection of the sky itself. The Ancient Ones were very fond of it. They said that it held a secret, but they loved it for its beauty only, and always carried a spray of it for good luck.'

'We have seen it,' said Aimi, 'not only on the ground, but on the national flag. I think the people must be very proud of it.'

Ranjee took the flower and threaded it into her hair. 'That is as may be, but how many of them know anything of its history? Or even know its name?'

They both shook their heads and looked at him expectantly as he sipped the last of his drink.

'This plant,' he continued at last, 'is one of the "rue" family, and is responsible for the name this country now goes by. Let me explain. When the first newcomers began to arrive here, one of them asked an Ancient what the place was called, pointing at the countryside as he did so. Well, the Ancient thought he was asking about the name of the flower, and the answer he gave was "pellaga-rue". "Pellaga", you see, is the old dialect word for "blue", so ever since then the country has been known as Pellagaroo.'

He smiled and winked at them. 'And I – I mean we – are probably the only ones who know that now.' He was silent for a while as though he was reflecting on the distant past.

'Ah yes,' he continued, rather sadly, 'the Ancient Ones. Such kind and simple people, but rich in their knowledge of the ways of nature. I worked with them for many years, grinding seeds into paste, extracting essences from petals, drying herbs and so forth, to help heal those who were unwell. Then, when the last of them fell away, things began to change, and not for the better. That is why I made my way up into the mountains and that is why I stayed – just as you see me now, content to be in the good company of innocent creatures, in the clean air, within the kingdom of the clouds.' He turned to the children who were both looking a little sad.

122

'Cheer up!' he said with a broad smile. 'There is a rhyme that those happy folk used to sing. Would you like to hear it?'

When they had both nodded eagerly, he stood up and began to dance around the room, singing in a soft, pleasant voice and gracefully waving his arms about:

The leaves of the saffo,
The fruit of the spry,
Are good for the hearing,
The heart and the eye.

Hot dandybean soup
Will improve the mind,
And also bring cheer
If the weather's unkind.

Chew tummel for toothache,
Eat oldmeg for warts.
Try worrybee seeds
If your blood's out of sorts.

The juice of the scab knot
If left to congeal
Is good for the skin
And helps wounds to heal.

Petals of bograin,
Roots of bugs-gore,
Berries of ossmane,
Stems of foxpoor...

These are the gifts
Kind Nature bestows,
For all kinds of ailments
And all sorts of woes.

But one little plant
Holds none of these powers.
It grows everywhere
With tiny blue flowers.

What is its secret,
What can it do,
This sky-coloured weed
Called pellaga-rue?

When he had finished his recital, Ranjee gave a little bow, as Dory and Aimi clapped their hands.

'Ranjee thanks you, and now I really think you should both get some sleep.'

He went across to Tamlin and began to talk to him, using the same foreign language and the same quick, nodding movements of his head, as he had before.

'I have told him not to be afraid of the smoke, which will soon be rising high,' he said. 'I know that he is troubled by fire. He told me when we first met – not in words, of course, but in a way that Ranjee understands. Now, off to bed with you, and tomorrow... well, we shall see what tomorrow will bring.'

From their dark corner of the room, the children watched as Ranjee piled dry twigs on the fire, and then sat cross-legged, carefully selecting and throwing one by one on to the fire the plants he had chosen earlier.

Each new addition to the flames produced smoke of a different colour, and these gradually intermingled to become a soft and beautiful shade of grey. The smoke seemed to linger for a while in front of Ranjee's eyes, swirling and dancing in fantastic shapes, before twisting into spirals and vanishing through the hole in the roof.

Chapter 14

Later in the night, Dory was awoken by the sound of glass jars clinking and saw, through sleepy eyes, the figure of Ranjee sorting through his collection of bottles and boxes. But the day had been a long and tiring one and soon sleep reclaimed him... and he was back at the breakfast table at home.

'Be careful,' his mother was saying, as she clung on to the table in an effort to stop herself being blown over by the wind that came rushing through the open window.

'Bit of a wind coming up!' shouted his father, as he flew out of the back door and over the garden wall. 'Carry you off, off, o-o-off!'

'Be careful,' repeated his mother, as the pots and pans followed his father out of the doorway. 'Don't take the kite, there's a good boy, good boy, good boy...'

'Good boy,' Aimi was saying as he opened his eyes. She was up before him as usual and she was talking to Tamlin as she prepared him for the journey ahead. 'Good boy,' she repeated, vigorously brushing his already gleaming coat. 'Whatever would we have done without you?'

Meanwhile, Ranjee was busy ladling out the breakfast porridge. 'It is a very nice morning to continue with your travelling. I am sorry that you are leaving so soon, but it is better that you set off when the day is still young and the sun is shining. No more fiery spirits, eh?'

They all laughed at this, but, as Aimi later pointed out, it was not so funny when they had first met the creatures and had run for their lives.

For a while they ate their meal in silence, the children now filled with unhappiness at the thought of parting company with this kind man who had proved to be such a good friend.

'I shall miss you both very much,' he said. 'So much so that I shall find it difficult to say goodbye.' He smiled his usual broad smile, but there was a sad look in his brown eyes and his head no longer nodded as he spoke.

'Last night's reading of the smoke,' he continued, as he poured out the tea, 'was a bit of a disappointment. The smoke does not lie, but I was hoping for at least a little more information. I sat before it for several hours, but the only clear message seemed so slight that I kept thinking that there must be more on the way, but it was not to be. Over and over again, I saw myself preparing a powder from the root of a certain plant and presenting it to you before you left my home.' He produced a small metal flask attached to a loop of cord. 'Guard it well,' he said, placing the loop over Dory's head and tucking the flask inside his shirt. 'I do not understand the meaning of this. Perhaps it is intended to be an amulet of some sort, a good luck charm that will protect you from harm as you continue with your quest. But I have done what the smoke required of me. Now we must let things take the course that Fate has laid out for them.'

'It is the pellaga-rue!' exclaimed Aimi. 'I just know it. That is what you made the powder from. I *am* right, aren't I?'

Ranjee raised his eyebrows in surprise at first. Then his expression turned to one of amusement.

'You could be right,' he said with a chuckle. 'You could well be right. But Ranjee can say no more.'

He gave them a bag containing some nuts and berries and a bottle of water. 'Take heed of these fruits, so that if you see them growing beside the path you will know they are safe to eat.'

'Don't you ever wish you could return home?' asked Dory, as he followed Ranjee and Aimi, who was leading Tamlin, out into the bright morning. 'I mean, your real home, the one that people here call the Other Side?'

The little man looked around him. Only the tops of the mountains could now be seen. They rose from out of a mist that completely blocked out the sight of anything below.

'Most days start like this,' he said. 'The morning mist turns the place into a land of cotton wool. It is very beautiful, but very dangerous, especially for the unwary. But it is a most suitable place for those who seek tranquillity and the great meaning of life. This is my home now and, besides, I could never leave my animals.'

He put his hand into the pocket of his robe and brought out a small brown bird. 'I found this little one a few weeks ago. It was lying on the track; I think it must have been trying to fly too soon.' He opened his fingers, but the bird made no attempt to fly away and just perched on the palm of his hand, preening its feathers. 'You see – it does not wish to leave me, so how could I leave it?'

He gave the bird to Aimi. 'Count to three and then let it go. Say "Go home, little bird", and be sure to watch where it goes as it flies away.'

This she did, but much to her surprise the bird did not fly off among the mountain peaks, but went straight up into the air, growing smaller and smaller until it finally disappeared.

'It has gone,' Aimi cried, 'but I do not think it has flown home – not unless it lives way up in the sky. Does it live up there, Ranjee?'

But there was no answer, and when they looked around, Ranjee was no longer there.

***

Although they were sad to leave the little man who had sheltered them when they had so desperately needed it and had treated them with such kindness, the children's mood gradually lifted as they rode further across the mountain. The sun had now burnt off the misty covering, making the way ahead clear and easy to ride on. Wild flowers and tall grasses grew on either side, and animals, mostly rabbit-like creatures, startled by the sound of Tamlin's hooves, ran this way and that while small, brightly coloured birds hopped among the bushes as they rode past, scolding them for being strangers.

Soon the track widened into a small road and began to dip among groups of trees that grew where parts of the mountainside had fallen away, giving unexpected glimpses of a new and faraway horizon of green hills.

'We could be in Blaggard territory, I suppose,' said Aimi. 'I wonder what their stronghold looks like. We must be getting close to them now, but hopefully we shall meet up with Sir Kitry and Sir Mons first.'

The thought of a confrontation with the Blaggards made Dory's heart quicken and he wondered what they should do if a group of them suddenly appeared. Perhaps now they should proceed with more caution, on foot even, or wait until evening before going any further.

'Do you think we ought to walk for a while?' Aimi asked, as if she had been reading his thoughts. 'We do not know how close we are to the Blaggards, or anyone else for that matter. It would not do for us to ride straight into danger. And, besides, my legs are getting a bit stiff, not to mention all my other bits. I expect Tamlin could do with a rest as well.'

They talked of Ranjee as they walked, recalling the strange and wonderful things they had seen him do with the plants and animals, and the magical effects he had produced from the smoke and what the meaning of the little flask was. And, while they agreed that it could be a charm for good fortune, which, Aimi pointed out, they needed as much of as they could get, on the other hand it was not a very scientific idea. Then, on reflection, they had to admit that there were lots of things in Pellagaroo that seemed like that – not scientific at all. And so they travelled on, chatting of all the things that had happened to them since their arrival, while Tamlin wandered ahead to graze wherever he saw patches of grass that were to his liking.

The next time the children looked up, they saw that the pony had stopped eating and was looking ahead with his neck arched and his ears pricked forwards.

'Whatever is wrong with him?' said Aimi. 'Not more goats, I hope.'

But it was not goats. Tamlin seemed more curious than frightened and began to step slowly towards what looked like a huge hole that was taking up most of the road ahead. Dory hurried forwards and grabbed the pony's bridle. He turned to Aimi. 'Hold on to him, while I take a closer look. The less weight we put on the ground, the better.' He moved cautiously towards the hole, crawling on hands and knees as he came closer, and then looked over the edge.

He could not believe his eyes at what he saw. The hole was very deep, and right at the bottom of it he saw the faces of Sir Kitry and Sir Mons looking up at him. At first, no one spoke, and then he heard Sir Mons shouting up at him.

'Great grizlings' blood! Dory, is that you?' he cried, his voice so loud that it made the sides of the hole shake. And then, when the amazed Dory failed to answer, Sir Kitry joined in, 'Dory, Dory, speak to us boy! We have fallen into a trap and cannot get ourselves out, try as we may, and... and... whatever are *you* doing here?'

Dory started to explain, but Sir Mons cut him short. 'Never mind all that now. Look, you have to get help. Ride back to Courtly Manor and tell them to send a couple of farm hands and one of the knights – Sir Kuss is the strongest – and a long length of very strong rope.'

Dory began to ask questions, but Sir Mons interrupted him again. 'Go now, as quickly as you can. I know it is a lot to ask of you, all that way back, but you are our only hope. Tell the squire what has happened, and tell the others to hurry back here. Off you go now, and good luck!'

Dory looked around and saw what Sir Kitry had meant about falling into a trap. Someone had obviously gone to a lot of trouble to conceal the hole with long, slender branches, leaves, dirt and pieces of turf, bits of which lay scattered around the hole.

'I'm on my way,' he shouted down the hole. 'And I'll be as quick as I can.'

But, when he turned to run back to Aimi, another shock was in store. Standing on either side of her were two of the strangest-looking people he had ever seen.

***

His first instinct was to run. The creatures were dressed in animal skins and their hair hung down over their shoulders. They carried long spears and around their necks were strings of beads and animal teeth.

They were both young, but the most striking thing about them was their size – each of them was about seven feet tall. 'Prehistoric' was the first word that came to Dory's mind. Great big prehistoric cavemen. But where on earth had they suddenly sprung from?

One of the men beckoned to him with a wave of his hand. 'Ookra,' he shouted, and then, when Dory hesitated, he beckoned again and repeated the word, 'Ookra, ookra!'

'Oh please do as he says,' begged a terrified Aimi. 'I do not understand a word they are saying, but they seem to want to take me – us – with them.'

Dory was very frightened, but he knew he could not leave Aimi on her own. Besides, both men looked as though they could quite easily catch him if he tried to run away.

'It's all right, Aimi,' he assured her, 'we'll just do whatever they want. We don't have any other choice. Perhaps when they realise we don't mean them any harm, they'll let us go.'

But, as he walked towards them, he felt the emptiness of the words ringing in his ears. How could it be all right? The men looked so fierce and Aimi so small and scared. The knights were trapped in a deep hole and depending on him to get help. The Professor was still a prisoner of the Blaggards and now he and Aimi had been captured by savages. Instead of things getting better, they were getting worse. Much worse!

Astride Tamlin once more, they were led back the way they had come, and then between some tall rocks, until they came to a natural stone archway leading to a large hole in the wall of the mountain. It was a tunnel, similar to the one that had led them into Ranjee's home, but much bigger. This took them to a vast, circular area that was surrounded by many smaller cave mouths and from these more of the strange beings now began to emerge. Some of them were men, who were even bigger than their captors, and some of them were women and children who now began to gather around them, jostling each other and reaching out, making Tamlin jerk his head up and down in alarm.

'I wish I knew what they were saying,' Aimi said, as the beings continued to jabber and touch them on their hands and hair, 'and that they would stop touching me.'

There now seemed to be an earnest discussion going on between the crowd and the two men who had brought them in. Once again the word 'ookra' was heard, repeated over and over again, until it was taken up by everyone and became a chant that even the cave-children joined in with. Their shouts of 'ookra, ookra, ookra!' filled the place with sound until the words gradually faded away to be replaced by a great buzz of excitement that went whispering around the walls and down into a hushed and expectant silence. Aimi looked around at the throng of faces that surrounded them. 'What are they going to do to us?' she cried. 'Oh, Dory, you were right. We should never have come up here on our own.'

Suddenly they were lifted off of Tamlin's back and carried through the now grinning and excited crowd of cavemen who made way for them, nodding and nudging each other as though they were sharing a pleasurable secret. Next, the children were placed in front of a large slab of stone, where they stood before the silent, wide-eyed creatures and looked at each other, both unable to speak due to the fear that the very worst was about to happen. But the crowd was not quiet for long. From out of one of the caves, two men now appeared, and a loud cheering broke out as they approached the slab and laid upon it a large coil of thick rope. They turned to the children and made a deep bow.

'Ookra,' they said, pointing to the rope, 'ookra, ookra.'

Dory and Aimi looked at each other in bewilderment. Whatever did it all mean? There was more talk between the men who had brought the rope, and much shrugging of shoulders, until someone in the crowd shouted something. And when it was realised that the children didn't understand their intentions, the men resorted to play-acting, tying one end of the rope around the waist of one of them, while the other pretended to pull him along. Next moment, Ami clasped her hands to her head with relief. 'Dory,' she shouted, as she realised what was happening, 'they do not want to hurt us at all! I think they are going to help us to rescue the knights!'

Dory looked at the faces around them and, now that the terrible fear that had gripped him was beginning to go away, he saw that the creatures he had assumed to be cruel savages were actually smiling. They were kind people who meant no harm. The word 'ookra' was probably their name for rope. He picked up the end of the coil and held it high. 'Ookra,' he said with a big smile, and 'ookra' was the crowd's immediate and happy response.

***

The rope, which the children now saw was made from vines woven skilfully together, was now picked up by one of the biggest of the men who hung it over his shoulder and walked out of the entrance tunnel, followed by Dory and Aimi and a sizeable group of the cave-dwellers.

'Hogga,' said the big man when they were all outside. He put the rope down, then struck his chest with his fist to indicate that it was his name. 'Hogga,' he said again, 'Hogga, Hogga.' He turned to the crowd. 'Gargants,' he shouted, sweeping his arm towards them and causing them all to laugh and shout the word back at him.

'Aimi,' said Dory, pointing at her. And then, tapping his own chest, 'Me, Dory.'

Hogga picked up the rope and, signalling the others to follow him, began to walk off in long, loping strides. But he had not gone more than twenty paces before he stopped as if he had forgotten something.

'Mee-do-ree,' he said, pointing a huge finger at Dory, 'Mee-do-ree, Mee-do-ree.' For some reason the words seemed to amuse him greatly, and he continued to repeat them at intervals, while smiling and shaking his head, until they reached the hole.

Hogga and the rest of the group now came to a halt, while Dory peered over the edge of the hole. 'Sir Mons,' he called out, 'Sir Kitry, can you hear me? It's me, Dory.'

The response was almost immediate. 'Dory,' he heard Sir Kitry say, 'whatever is going on? Surely you cannot have been to the farm already! Is Tamlin lame? Are you all right? Where is Aimi?'

'It's a long story,' Dory replied, when he managed at last to get a word in. 'There's a rope coming down to you in a minute. Tie it around your waist and, when you're ready, you'll be pulled up. I'll explain afterwards.'

Sir Kitry came up first and his reaction was one of astonishment. 'What the... why... whoever are these... people?'

Sir Mons was just as surprised. 'I have heard of giants once living in the area,' he said, after Dory had told them what had happened. 'Stories of huge footprints being discovered along the riverbanks, giant bones being dug up by farmers ploughing, that sort of thing. But I never thought any of it was true.'

The Gargants stood quietly by, smiling and shuffling their feet, and once again Dory saw how very different they were from the wild and warlike beings he had first imagined. They were actually quite shy and childlike, and now they seemed reluctant to stay, waving their hands from time to time and quickly edging away in the direction of their home.

'I wish I could thank them,' Aimi said, as Hogga smiled and began to turn away.

'We shall not forget you,' said Sir Kitry, as both he and Sir Mons raised their hands in salute.

'Thank you,' added Sir Mons. 'for saving us.' Hogga nodded as if he understood what had been said and then, with a final wave, he joined the others.

Dory wanted to shout after them, to tell them in their own language how much they owed to them. When they were almost out of sight, he called out the only word he knew they would understand, 'Ookra! Ookra!' But only Hogga seemed to have heard him, for without turning around he lifted the coil of rope high above his head in a silent farewell.

'Goodbye!' said Aimi, as they disappeared from view. 'I am sorry that I thought you were bad people.'

'And I thought that they were the ones who had dug the hole,' added Dory. 'Well, until I got to know them better, that is.'

The knights now began to pick bits of twigs and leaves out of their armour.

'Are you both all right?' asked Aimi. 'That hole was very deep.'

'I have a few dents here and there,' Sir Kitry replied, 'but otherwise I am undamaged. Nothing that cannot be put right later on.'

Sir Mons pointed to his chest. 'I have a squashed breastplate, where someone – I mention no names – fell on top of me, but I suppose it could have been worse!'

The ground on both sides of the hole was quite firm and safe to walk on. Sir Mons went first, then Sir Kitry, with the children leading Tamlin.

'I wonder who did dig the hole,' Aimi said, as she climbed on to Tamlin's back. 'Could it have been the Blaggards?'

Sir Kitry shook his head. 'Nobody dug it. The hole is the result of a natural fall of rock, a subsidence down below that must have happened many years ago. But somebody took a lot of trouble to carefully cover it over until it looked like solid ground. It made the perfect trap.'

Sir Mons nodded. 'Which we fell into! Blaggards have been at work again. We must be getting near to their headquarters now, so everyone on their guard. They are sure to have a lookout posted somewhere along the way.'

Chapter 15

It was Sir Kitry who spotted him first. 'Don't look now. Just keep talking and acting naturally. There is a Blaggard on a high ledge about fifty yards ahead to our left. He has just dodged behind a big rock, but I am sure he is still there.'

'He must not be allowed to escape to warn the others,' said Sir Mons. 'He cannot hurt us otherwise, and I can pick him off if we can just get a little closer.'

It was difficult for the children not to look up as they drew nearer, but they managed to keep up a conversation with each other until they heard Sir Kitry's warning.

'There he goes, Captain! Quick, he is making a run for it.'

There was a sudden flash of firepower and they saw the black shape of the lookout duck, and then jump from one ledge to another as the rock face above his head splintered into pieces.

'Missed him!' muttered Sir Mons angrily. 'Come on, Kit, we have to find him.'

Below the ledge where the Blaggard had been perched was a series of large boulders, piled one upon the other, which provided a ready-made stairway to the lookout spot. Sir Kitry pointed to one of the boulders. 'See that black smudge of paint? He must have slipped and fallen and that is where he bounced off the rock. He must still be here somewhere. We would have seen him if he had managed to run away.'

A further search revealed what had happened. There was a gully at the base of the stones, not much more than a small ditch in size, and the Blaggard had fallen into it and was now tightly wedged in a cleft at the bottom.

'Is he, is he... dead?' Dory asked as he arrived at the scene. One of the Blaggard's arms twitched and creaked and a faint bleeping sound came from his helmet. The knights looked at each other and neither spoke for a moment.

'Our kind do not die,' said Sir Kitry at last. 'Well, not in the sense that you mean.'

'No,' said Sir Mons, 'but we can be put out of action.' He pointed a finger at the Blaggard's head, but before he could release the firepower, Sir Kitry placed a hand on his arm.

'Hold on, Captain, do not waste your fire.' He lay down, reached into the gully, pressed the top of the Blaggard's helmet down, gave it a quick twist and then carefully lifted it off.

'Now, let me see,' he muttered, picking through the bundle of wires inside the head and then plucking a couple out of their connections. He waited for the bleeping sounds to end and the arm to stop moving and then replaced the top of the helmet. 'Good. That should do the trick.'

They piled small rocks over the body until it was completely covered.

'If he is lucky,' Sir Kitry said, 'he will be discovered one day and a screwdriver and a few hours of daylight will put him right. Perhaps by then he will have learned some good manners!' Then he added, '"Not dead, only sleeping." Isn't that what you humans say?'

Sir Mons shook his head and burst out laughing. 'Those people at the old Zimco factory where you were made have much to answer for. You are far too sentimental for your own good!'

**

Although now having reached the opposite side of the mountain, they were prevented from seeing the land below, hemmed in as they were by a seemingly continuous ridge of stone which sloped up from the side of the track, its surface smooth and hard and impossible to climb.

'We must be very close now,' said Sir Mons. 'If only we could look out over that ridge, we might see something that would give us a clue and save us from being caught off guard.'

Dory pointed ahead. 'I think I can see a place where the surface of the ridge isn't so smooth. Look, there are cracks in it with grass and small bushes growing out of them. I'm quite a good climber. I bet I could get to the top and take a look over the edge.'

Sir Mons nodded. 'Yes, I see where you mean. Let us take a closer look.'

'It is not so steep here, Captain,' called Sir Kitry, as they considered Dory's suggestion. 'The clumps of grass would give him a bit of a foothold and the bushes look like they could be strong enough for him to hang on to.'

'And we could catch him if he were to tumble backwards,' Sir Mons added, turning to Dory.

'You know, I think it is a good idea. Well worth a try, but remember not to give the game away. It is very important that you are not seen. *Very* important!'

He lifted Dory up and placed him on to the bottom of the ridge. 'Have a good look around. See if you can spot any buildings, or detect any signs of movement, and remember to keep your voice down.'

Dory edged his way up the slope and was soon peering cautiously over the top. 'I can see some of the base of the mountain,' he called down quietly. 'There are doors and windows cut into the rock. It looks as if the track we're on winds right down to it.'

He was quiet for a moment or two, and then said, 'I can't see anyone, but I think I can hear voices.'

He leaned out to get a better view. 'Yes, I can just...' but before he could say any more, the shrub he had been holding on to came right out of the ground and, with a gasp of fright, he fell over the edge.

***

'Dory!' cried Aimi, as he vanished from sight. She looked at the knights. '*Do* something!' she pleaded. 'Please, please do something!'

But Dory had been lucky, at least at first. Directly below the spot he had fallen from was another track. It was a much narrower one, but one that jutted out far enough to save him from disaster. He stood up and saw, apart from a bruise or two, how very fortunate he had been. There was a sheer drop of perhaps a hundred feet to the ground below and the shock of seeing it made him feel so dizzy that he quickly had to sit down again.

There were figures moving about down there, knights wearing black armour – his first sight of the dreaded Blaggards in their stronghold – and one of them only had to look up and see him and 'the game', as Sir Mons had called it, would be well and truly given away. There was no way he could climb back up – it was too steep – and, anyway, he would almost surely have been seen from below. He decided to crawl further along the path in the hope that somewhere ahead he might find a way back to join Aimi and the knights who must surely now believe that he had fallen to his death.

A shadow passed over him and he saw a grizling swoop lazily down to the ground and waddle unconcerned among the Blaggards, throwing its head back and making the most awful croaking sound until pieces of meat were brought out and fed to it. It was a truly horrible scene, but not as bad as what he saw next. From around the corner of the rock face, two Blaggards were rapidly advancing on him, while from above he could hear Aimi's cries of anguish. It was bad enough that he was now about to be captured, but if they heard *her* the whole trip would probably have been in vain. There was only one thing he could think of to do. Still on his hands and knees, and pretending that he hadn't seen the Blaggards, he began to sing at the top of his voice the words of his school song:

In the bright morning
Of our lives,
Eager to learn, eager to play,
So each one strives
To do the very best
That hearts and minds can...

'Stand up boy!' he heard a harsh voice command. 'And stop making that awful noise.' In front of him he saw four black metal legs which ended in sharply pointed boots that were so close to his face that he could see the rows of rivets that held them together.

'Stand up!' the order came again, and when he was slow in carrying it out, he felt a hand take hold of his hair and pull him painfully to his feet. Both of the Blaggards' visors lifted at the same time and two pairs of steely grey eyes glared down at him.

'Well, I'll be a rusty bucket!' said the Blaggard who had pulled him to his feet. 'What do we have here? What do you make of it, Mister Donno?'

The other considered the question as he looked Dory up and down. 'It is very strange, whatever it is, Mister Prank. When I first heard the noise it was making, I thought it was one of our grizlings wanting its dinner. But this is no grizling, Mister Prank, because *they* do not crawl around on their hands and knees. I reckon it is trying to fool us. I reckon it is one of those humans – you know, one of those creatures that thought they were going to rule over us and make the Black Guards their servants. I don't *think* so!'

The Blaggard, Prank, turned Dory's head so that he could look down over the edge. 'Do you see that black bird down there, boy?' he whispered. Dory tried to nod, while Prank continued in the same quiet, sinister voice. 'If you were to fall from this height, your puny body would smash into jelly – a perfect meal ready for it to feast on.' He tightened his grip on Dory's hair and swung him over the edge at arm's length.

'Shall I let go of you boy,' he asked, bobbing him up and down, 'as a special treat for my little pet?' But there was no answer from Dory. This final act had been too much for him and he had fainted from sheer terror. Prank dropped his limp body on to the path.

'Pick him up,' he said to his companion. 'There is something very odd going on here. We had better see what the General has to say about it.'

Meanwhile, Sir Kitry, who had been trying to climb up the slope on the other side and finding it very difficult due to his considerable weight and metal boots, had finally made it to the top and was just in time to see Dory's body being carried away.

'They've got him!' he called down to the others. 'Those monsters have captured Dory!'

***

When Dory regained consciousness, he saw that they were now approaching the stronghold. Donno put him down. 'You can walk from now on. But try to run and I shall cut both your ears off!'

There were Blaggards going in and out of the main entrance and others looked down at him from the windows above, all giving him the same cold stare. How different, he thought, from Sir Kitry and Sir Mons. How he wished he was walking with them and not these unfeeling, mechanical beings who seemed to enjoy being cruel.

The grizling was still in front of the stronghold, tearing at lumps of raw meat with its huge talons and blood-covered beak, but it stopped feeding as Dory went past, cocking its head on one side and regarding him knowingly and curiously. The boy wondered if this was one of the birds that Sir Kitry had fired at, and if, perhaps, it recognised him.

Close by were other entrances, simple square doorways cut from the mountainside, and from these came the sounds of hammering, as chisels struck stone, and the ring of metal on metal. They stood and waited as a line of human workers shuffled past with their heads down, and one of their guards met Dory's gaze and drew a finger across his own throat as a sign of what might be about to happen.

'Prank and Donno at your service,' shouted Donno when he saw the guard's gesture. 'We catch them, you dispatch them – you have it easy!'

At the entrance, Dory was handed over to two new guards who wore red armbands bearing the sign of the Black Grizling, and these quickly escorted him to a small room that was completely empty of furniture.

'Remember to treat the General with the utmost respect when he decides to send for you,' said one of the guards as he locked him in. 'And if you know what is good for you, do not lie to him.'

Dory sat on the floor in a corner of the room and tried hard to think of an excuse for being on the mountain so close to the Blaggards' headquarters, but an hour later, when the two guards returned for him, his mind was still empty.

'What now?' said a voice that he hardly recognised as his own. He remembered Sir Kitry's warning: 'General Madza – avoid at all costs.'

***

'Dash my cogs and wiring!' exclaimed Sir Mons, when Sir Kitry had slithered and clambered back down on to the track. 'Whatever was I thinking of to let that boy climb up there? Now he is in the hands of the enemy. I should be reduced to the ranks, I really should.'

He looked down at Aimi's worried face. 'I am sorry,' he said more quietly, 'but failing to protect a human, and a young human at that, is something that just should not happen.'

Aimi hauled herself up on to Tamlin's back and for a moment the knights thought that she was about to ride off without them. Her voice was determined and calm.

'Dory said that this path leads right down to the fortress, didn't he? Can we now go and rescue him, please? It is all my fault. I am the one who got him involved in all this. *Please*, we have to do *something*!'

Sir Mons drew himself up to his full height. 'Of course. No use blaming ourselves. Action is what is needed now. Come on. We can make plans as we go and finalise things when we have had a good look at the lie of the land.'

'Now, Kit, what did you see down there? Any ground cover that we can use? Blaggards patrolling around? Sentries at the main entrance?'

Chapter 16

The General's office was situated at the top of a flight of stone stairs, the sides of which were hung with red banners all bearing the now familiar emblem of the black bird. Blaggards marched past them in the corridor as Dory and his escorts stood waiting to be admitted, while an elderly worker, pushing a trolley loaded with mops and buckets, passed them by without looking up.

From inside the office, the sound of voices, muffled by the thick wooden door, came mumbling out in an annoying buzz. Although one voice in particular became raised at times, none of the words was clear enough to be understood. Then, as the conversation died away and he felt his escorts stiffen and stand up straight on either side of him, Dory saw the door swing open and heard the command 'Enter!'

Inside were more banners and smaller flags, and hanging on the wall behind the General's desk was a large map of what looked like the country of Pellagaroo, together with various items of weaponry.

'Now, young man,' said the General quietly and soothingly, 'you seem to be in a spot of bother.'

He was a big Blaggard, almost as big as Sir Mons, and he wore a tall helmet with black feathers at the top while a shiny metal image of a grizling hung from a chain around his neck. He leaned forwards, rested his elbows on his desk and clasped his hands together. 'Two of my guards,' he nodded in the direction of Prank and Donno who stood with some others at the back of the room, 'seem to think that you are some kind of threat to us, but I cannot believe that. You seem to me to be a nice young man – for a human, that is. Now, tell me just what you are doing up here, on my mountain, so close to my little establishment.'

When Dory didn't reply, he continued, 'I think I know why you are here. No doubt you had heard of the great General Madza, and decided to visit him for a chat and a cup of tea. Was that it?' Dory tried to answer, but his mouth had now completely dried up and seemed to have stopped working. In desperation, he managed a small nod.

'What is the matter?' asked the General, his voice now little more than a whisper, 'Grizling got your tongue?'

There was a snigger of laughter from the back of the room and the General immediately leapt to his feet and slammed his fist on to the desk.

'Silence!' he shouted, pointing his finger at Donno. 'Another sound from you and you will be deprived of three months' daylight.' He then turned his attention back to Dory. 'Now,' he said, dropping his voice again to a whisper, 'would you like a nice piece of cake and a cup of tea?'

Dory nodded and managed to find his voice again. 'Yes please, sir. I would like that very much.'

'And you shall have them, just as soon as you tell me who it was who brought you here so that you could pretend to be a little lost boy! Who thought it would be a clever idea for my guards to bring you into the Great Madza's domain so we would think you were no more than a wandering innocent who crawls on his hands and knees and sings to himself, someone who is dismissed as having a few wires missing, or a loose cog, and is then released to tell my enemies all about what he has seen here?'

'But I was lost, sir,' pleaded Dory, seizing on the General's remarks, 'and I wasn't spying on you. I didn't know it was your mountain, I really didn't. And I didn't know it was your... your domain. I'm really sorry, sir, and I promise that I'll never do it again.'

The General stood up. 'You are right, you will not. You will *never* do it again.' He pointed at Prank and Donno. 'You are the ones who found him, so you are the ones I am handing him back to. Find one of the senior officers and tell him the boy is a spy and my orders are that he is to be put in a cell, searched and interrogated. Lose him and they will be picking you both up with a brush and a shovel!'

***

'Now you're for it,' said Prank, as they marched Dory away.

'And that is for getting me into trouble with the General,' added Donno, giving him a push in the back that sent him sprawling. 'You dirty little spy!'

There was a group of Blaggards nearby and one of them came over and spoke to the guards.

'What is all this about?' he asked, as Dory was getting to his feet. 'Who is this boy?'

'He is a spy, sir,' replied Prank.

'General Madza's orders, sir,' added Donno. 'He is to be put into a cell and searched and questioned by a senior officer. Can you spare the time, sir, or should we ask one of the other officers?'

The Blaggard stared down at Dory. 'I hate spies,' he said. 'Put him in cell 13 and I shall get to him as soon as I can.'

Cell 13 turned out to be a damp-walled room at the far end of a line of cells below ground level. A stone slab and two blocks of wood served as table and chairs.

'Can I have a drink of water, please?' begged Dory, when the officer arrived. 'I'm so tired and thirsty.'

He sat down and rested his head on the stone table. 'I just want a drink of water and to go to sleep.'

The officer placed his hands on the table and looked down at him. 'No!' he shouted, 'You cannot. Not until you confess what you have been up to.'

He turned away and stood with his back to Dory and looked out through the bars of the cell door.

'Sit up straight,' he said sharply, and then, much more quietly, 'Look at the back of my right arm. Has anyone ever told you of a Black Guard who bears a firepower battle scar like that?'

Deep in Dory's weary mind, a memory began to stir, and suddenly he was wide awake and able to recall what Sir Kitry had told him about the Loyal Protector who was an agent, a spy with the sign of a scorch mark. He looked at the officer's arm and saw a strange discolouration there. It was a jagged scar that looked as if a miniature bolt of lightning had struck it, burning away the black paint and revealing the shining metal that lay beneath. A glimmer of hope rose up inside him. Perhaps his luck was about to change. Or was it all some kind of trick? After a while, the officer turned back to face him.

'Obviously not,' he said. 'Not that the mark means anything, anyway.'

'Someone did once tell me of such a *knight*,' said Dory cautiously. 'But what they said might not be true.'

The officer sat down opposite him. 'Can you describe the person who told you that,' he asked, 'the one who told you the story that might not be true? What did they look like?'

'He was very kind,' replied Dory, 'and he had bright blue eyes, and he had a friend, a big friend with one eye as black as a piece of coal.'

The officer leaned forward. 'Sir Kitry?' he whispered, 'and Sir Mons, also known as Captain Coaleye?'

Dory hesitated. The thought that this might turn out to be some kind of trap, one that might endanger not only himself, but Sir Kitry, Sir Mons and Aimi as well, returned to him and would not go away.

***

There was a long silence as they looked at each other across the table. Then the visor on the officer's helmet moved up and down several times in quick succession. When it lifted for the last time Dory saw that his eyes were now as sparkling and as blue as Sir Kitry's.

'Now do you trust me?' he asked. 'I am Sir Tanty, a true Loyal Protector, but here I am known as Captain Dalgo. You had better tell me what is going on.'

Hurriedly, Dory told Sir Tanty about the capture of Aimi's father, how the two knights had set out to rescue him and that they and Aimi were close by and probably unsure of what to do next. Sir Tanty nodded. 'I have seen her father,' he said. 'He works in the laboratory. They watch him night and day. It is a difficult situation because, rather than let him be rescued, they would put him to the sword.'

There were footsteps now at the end of the corridor and Sir Tanty shot up and began to raise his voice.

'You *will* tell me!' he shouted. 'And if you do not, I shall feed you alive to the grizlings! Have you any idea what that would feel like? First they will peck out your eyes, then they will tear out your liver, and all the while you will be wishing you could hurry up and die. Is that what you want?'

He peered out of the cell and then sat down again. 'Sorry about that,' he whispered, 'but I have to make it look real. Look, do you have anything on you that might incriminate you, anything that you should not have? I am supposed to search and interrogate you, so I have to play the part, much as I hate doing it.'

Dory turned out his pockets and placed a small magnet, the torch, a glass marble and the stub of a pencil on the table.

'That's all I have,' he said. 'Oh, and this as well.' He pulled the little flask that Ranjee had given him out from under his shirt. 'It's full of a powder given to us by a man called Ranjee. He's a kind of a mystic man, a hermit who lives in a cave up on the mountain. He seems to be able to see things, important messages that appear to him in the smoke of his fire when certain plants are burnt on it. Anyway, he said that the smoke had told him to prepare a powder made from the root of a certain plant and to give it to us when we left him. He told me to be sure not to lose it.'

Sir Tanty held up the flask by its cord and examined it closely. 'Did he tell you which plant the powder was made from?'

'He wouldn't say, but Aimi made a guess that it was the blue flower that's on the Pellagaroon flag. I think it was a pretty good guess because he just smiled and wouldn't deny it.'

Sir Tanty got up and once again peered out through the bars of the cell door. 'And,' he said, when he had resumed his seat, 'what were you to use it for, this powder?'

'I don't think Ranjee knew. He told us that the messages he received often didn't tell the full story and that all he'd been given were instructions to make the powder and then give it to us. Aimi and I wondered if it might be just a good luck charm. Maybe that's all it is.'

'And maybe not,' said Sir Tanty, handing the flask back to him. 'Put it away now in case someone sees it. I have to think about this.'

***

They sat in near silence as Sir Tanty considered all that he had just been told. Meanwhile, Dory listened to the faint riffle of sound, as though someone was flicking through a deck of cards, that came from somewhere within the knight's body.

'Thank Zimco for my memory file,' said Sir Tanty, at length. 'I had almost forgotten the legend of the little blue weed.'

There was shouting now, further down the corridor, and then the clang of a cell door being shut.

'Quick!' hissed Sir Tanty, as the sound of footsteps drew nearer. 'Get down on your knees and look as terrified as you can.'

'Everything all right, sir?' asked a guard, peering into the cell. 'I can give you a hand if you like. I am a really good persuader, I am, sir. I can...'

Sir Tanty whirled around to face him. 'Go away, you fool! Can you not see that the prisoner is just ready to break? If you have ruined things I shall see that the General himself knows about it and you shall soon be flying off the top of the mountain. Go away and stay away!'

He waited until the guard's hurried footsteps faded away and then turned back to Dory.

'It seems,' he continued, as though nothing had happened, 'that many, many years ago the original people who lived here were very fond of the little blue flower. There was even some kind of prophecy that, one day, it would come to their aid if the need was great enough. That is probably why it was used as a national emblem. Later generations came to dismiss it all as no more than a romantic story, and now most folk know nothing of its history at all.'

'Do you think there could be a connection,' asked Dory, 'with that old prophecy and this flask of powder?'

'It does seem a bit far-fetched, I admit, but my memory was also jogged by something else. Do you know what Damaric Water is?' Dory nodded.

'Well, years later, when the Zimco team were in the process of developing it, a rumour began to spread about one of the experiments. It showed, so the story goes, that a substance obtained from a certain plant, if added in even the tiniest amount to the Damaric Water, would destroy its wonderful life-giving powers. It would make it useless and very dangerous if used on knights. It would cause them to stop functioning, or, in human terms, to die.'

'What was the name of the plant? Does anybody know?'

Sir Tanty shook his head. 'No, but possibly it was hushed up, because it was generally agreed by those concerned that it was the blue flower shown on the national flag and that it would not do to have that labelled as a possible knight-killer. Put all these things together and you begin to see a picture emerging. Perhaps your arrival here is not entirely due to chance. Supposing some power for good is using you and the man Ranjee to fulfil that old promise and that the little flask is the weapon that will bring the Blaggards down, once and for all!'

***

There was a small jar of candlemoss in a corner of the cell and now its light began to fade.

'There is a light at the end of the corridor,' said Sir Tanty, seeing Dory's anxious look, 'so you will not be completely in the dark. Now, please listen. I have a plan and it includes you. It is a big gamble, so if you do not want to be a part of it I shall understand. It is based on what we have just been talking about. As you may know, the Blaggards do not possess many of the advantages that the Loyals have. They have no firepower, thank goodness, nor do they have any capacity for pity, kindness and so on, but they also lack an inbuilt system of Damaric Water – a refinement that came into being after they had broken away to become Black Guards. Consequently, they have to take a weekly dose, a small but vital cupful, which is handed out at a morning parade organised by one of the junior officers.'

Dory looked puzzled. 'Do you mean they *drink* it?'

Sir Tanty shook his head. 'No, not in the way humans do. They tip it in through their voiceboxes. It is a bit crude, but it gets into their systems and that is what matters.' Anyway, by great good fortune, this week's Damaric parade is to be held tomorrow morning. It takes place in a large room just above these cells. At the far end of the room is a tank holding the Damaric Water. Now, if the contents of your flask could be added to that water some time before morning, I believe – given what I now know – that it will do considerable damage to those who take a dose of it. I *have* to believe that! And that is where you come in.'

He looked at Dory for his reaction and, when he saw his firm nod of the head, continued, 'I shall come to see you about an hour or so before the parade. Try to get some sleep before then. I shall make some excuse to the guardroom about waking you up just for the fun of it – they will like that – but when I return the keys I shall leave your cell door unlocked. The rest is up to you. Go very quietly and watch out for any patrolling guards. Only make a move when you think it is safe. Look for the room – you will see a sign on the door that says "Damaric parade today". Go into the room, lift the lid of the tank, shake in all of the powder and *do not* leave the flask behind to be found. Get back to the cell as quickly as you can without being spotted and then close the cell door. If ever the old legend was really meant to come true, the time is surely now. If not, well, things will not look so good for you and me!'

Dory tried to smile. 'They've got it in for me, anyway, so I'll try my best to do as you say.'

'Try to get some sleep,' repeated Sir Tanty. 'Hopefully, tomorrow will turn out to be a great day for us all.'

There was the sound of the door being locked and Dory sat in the gloom listening to the knight's footsteps echoing away down the corridor and up the stone steps into the silence of the night. He lay across the table and cradled his head in his arms. He was worried and scared about what would soon be happening, but he was also very tired and soon was well asleep. For a few short hours his rest was thankfully deep and dreamless, until a slight noise like someone coughing or perhaps a mouse skittering across the floor made him open his eyes in alarm. Why was it so dark? Where was everyone? Where was he? And then the grizling settled down on him, smothering him with its wings and closing its claws on him.

Chapter 17

'Get off me!' he cried. 'Let me go!' But the presence was dark and would not move, until he recognised Sir Tanty's reassuring voice and felt his hand gently stirring him out of his nightmare into full wakefulness.

'I have brought you some water,' he heard the knight whisper. 'Take your time in drinking it. Remember what the plan is? Leave the cell about fifteen minutes after me. The corridor is now in darkness, but there is a light burning at the bottom of the stairs. If you do meet a guard, your only hope is to make a run for it. You never know, you might find your way back to Sir Kitry and company.'

'But what about you?' asked Dory. 'What will you do then?'

'Me? Well, if they have not found me out, I shall go back to pretending to be the wicked Captain Dalgo, and bide my time.'

He paused at the cell door. 'Good luck, young man. And keep a sharp lookout for those guards.'

Alone again, Dory drank the last of the water and considered his next few moves. It seemed simple enough, just so long as he didn't get caught. But would the powder really work in the way that Sir Tanty had suggested? He waited until he guessed fifteen minutes had passed and then left the cell. It was all or nothing now!

There was, as Sir Tanty had said, a light at the bottom of the stairs, so he waited in the gloom of the passage listening carefully for the sound of any approaching guards before daring to step out and dart quickly up the steps. Right in front of him was the door with the sign hanging on it and he was inside the room standing before the Damaric tank, hardly able to believe his luck, within two minutes of leaving his cell. It had all been so easy – not a guard in sight. He was alone in the room and now all he had to do was tip in the powder, get back to the cell and wait for the result.

The metal tank was large and he had to stretch up in order to reach the lid. As he did so, he felt a slight tremor from inside, a ripple of movement that vibrated against his hand. He remembered how the liquid had swirled around so mysteriously at Castle Gardemal and how Gully had said something about it being alive, and for a moment he felt that there was someone near, or at least a presence of some kind, in the room with him. He unscrewed the top of the flask, cautiously lifted the lid of the tank and poured the powder in. To his dismay, the sudden reaction from inside – a sharp, fierce whine of sound and then a bubbling up of the liquid – made the flask slip from his fingers and fall into the tank as well. Now the Damaric Water began to move around even more, splashing and churning as though a shoal of fish was writhing about in it, and the tank shuddered so much that he fully expected the guards to rush in to see what was going on. Then gradually all sounds of movement ceased and he heard a quiet groan, followed by a long, sad sigh, as the lid of the tank fell shut and the presence he had felt earlier, whether real or imagined, disappeared.

Suddenly, there were noises from outside, the unmistakable clatter of metal boots and the harsh voices of two or more Blaggards rang through passages and then stopped outside the doorway. There was laughter, and then someone said 'You had better have a quick check, just in case.'

Frantically, Dory looked around for somewhere to hide.

***

It was dark now on the sixth peak as a rather tired Aimi and her companions descended the mountain trail. Lower down, the path had narrowed and ran through patches of woodland where the wayside was conveniently covered in thick grass that muffled the sound of their footsteps. As usual, it was Aimi who was the first to sense that trouble lay near. Reining the pony to a halt, she motioned the knights to silence.

'Voices,' she whispered. 'I thought I could hear voices ahead.'

'You had better take a look, Kit,' said Sir Mons in the silence that followed. 'There are sure to be sentries posted soon.'

After Sir Kitry had disappeared through the trees, Aimi and Sir Mons heard someone say, 'I would not want to be in that brat's boots. I wonder what old Feather-top has got planned for him?'

'Stick his head on a pole?'

'Feed him to a grizzle-guts?'

'Whatever it is, let us hope it does not happen until we are off duty. I would hate to miss all the fun!'

This exchange was followed by much wild laughter, which continued after Sir Kitry had returned.

'Blaggards,' he whispered urgently, 'under some trees not far ahead. I could not see much, but I do not think there are more than two of them. It is probably too close to the stronghold to risk using firepower, but I have been thinking. If I could somehow lure them back here – and I believe I can – do you suppose we could deal with them? Quietly, I mean?'

Sir Mons was quick to agree. 'Do it. We cannot afford to waste any more time. We may be too late as it is. Get on with it however you can. Aimi and I will hide in the bushes.'

Sir Kitry chose the darkest spot he could find, and lay down in the long grass.

'Help,' he cried in a weak voice. 'Help, I need help.'

The guards' laughter stopped at once, and a shout came out of the darkness.

'Who is that? Step forward and be recognised!'

'I am the lookout,' called Sir Kitry, faintly. 'I have had a fall. I need treatment. You will have to carry me in and find a replacement.'

More muttering came from the suspicious guards, and Sir Kitry cried out again. 'Help me, please. I have crawled all the way from the lookout post. I cannot last much longer. I am losing Damaric fast.'

Almost immediately came the sound of bodies hurrying through the undergrowth as the Blaggards followed the direction of the knight's groans.

'All right, all right,' muttered one of them, gruffly, 'don't make such a fuss. You take one of his arms, Bucky, while I grab the other. Heave ho! But as they were about to lift the knight's body, each felt an iron grip on the back of his neck.

'Take that!' growled Sir Mons, as he banged their heads together. 'I will give you "head on a pole", you pair of malsprockets.'

He looked at Sir Kitry and then at the dazed Blaggards, who were lying on the grass, their bodies twitching helplessly and their voices squealing and stuttering nonsense at high speed.

'Do your trick with the wiring, Kit,' he added, 'and let us be on our way.'

***

There was a small space behind the tank and Dory managed to squeeze himself into it just as the door was being opened. A moment passed, then the door was closed again, but the sound of the voices, although fainter now, continued as the guards lingered nearby.

Dory squeezed himself further still into the gap behind the tank, his back and his knees now beginning to ache. Soon, it seemed as though the space was getting smaller and he found it difficult to breathe. But the voices now increased in number and, before long, he heard the door open again and the sound of cups being laid out in readiness for the parade.

'Line up in order of rank,' someone shouted when the Blaggards began to crowd into the room. 'General

Madza will start the ceremony just as soon as he arrives.'

'Ah, there you are, sir. Good morning, sir. Damaric all ready for you, sir,' continued the voice.

'To the Black Guards!' Dory heard the General say as he tipped his head back and poured in the liquid.

'To the Black Guards!' came the reply from the rest of the company.

And so it continued, from guard to guard, until someone interrupted the proceedings. 'Captain Dalgo, sir, you have not had your Damaric. Make way for the Captain!'

There were a few moments of silence, as though Sir Tanty had hesitated, and then Dory heard someone say, 'What *is* the matter, Dalgo? You must not go without your Damaric, unless of course, you feel ready for the scrapyard!'

There was laughter from the rest of the group, and Dory held his breath as he wondered what would happen next.

'To the Black Guards!' cried Sir Tanty. 'Long live the Black Guards!' There was a cheer at this from the crowd remaining and then the ceremony continued until the last toast was drunk and the room was empty once more.

Poor Sir Tanty, thought Dory, as he wondered if the knight had realised that he, too, would have to drink the now possibly harmful Damaric Water.

Painfully and stiffly, Dory wriggled out of his hiding place and stepped back into the room. Half of him hoped that the powder would turn out to be a failure, while the other half hoped it would work in the way that Sir Tanty wished. Meanwhile, he had to try to get back to his cell without being seen. Carefully listening and watching out for any guards, he quickly ran down the steps, back through the passage and into the darkness of his cell. With a deep sigh of relief, he closed the door and sat down. But, suddenly, there was a scrape of metal on stone and, too late, he realised that he was not alone.

'Well, well, I do believe our little bird has returned to his nest. Been for a walk, have we?' said Donno.

***

The General appeared to be deep in thought as Dory was brought before him. His head was down and he tapped his fingers on his desk, over and over again, as if perhaps he was trying to control his temper before he spoke. He lifted his head at last and, although his gaze was steady and his voice calm, Dory was alarmed to see the tips of the feathers on the General's helmet begin to tremble, as though to signal an approaching storm.

'Now,' he said, in the same quiet, menacing way that Dory had become used to, 'let us get this over and done with quickly. Who let you out of your cell? Was it someone you can see in this room? If you can identify him, I promise I will deal with you leniently.'

Dory gazed at the guards who were gathered around the walls of the General's office and was relieved to see Sir Tanty, who was staring out in the same grim, steely-eyed way as all the others, showing him no sign of recognition. He looked back at the General and shook his head.

'Speak up!' said the General, his voice now louder. 'Can you see who it was?'

'No sir, no one helped me. I tried the cell door and it was unlocked. I got out because I just wanted to go home. I saw that I couldn't escape, so I went back to my cell.'

The General went back to tapping his fingers. 'You are a liar! And you should never lie to me, as anyone here will testify.'

His eyes swept around the room until they settled on Sir Tanty. 'Captain Dalgo will now step forward and face the prisoner.'

The General turned back to Dory. 'Tell me,' he said, 'have you ever seen this officer before?'

Dory thought quickly before answering. 'Yes, sir. He asked me lots of questions yesterday, and then again last night when he woke me up. But I couldn't tell him anything because I don't really know anything, sir.'

Now the General's voice grew even louder. 'So, Captain, you were the last person to visit this boy in his cell. You then returned the keys to the guardroom and the cell was later found to have been left unlocked. What have you got to say about that?'

Sir Tanty came smartly to attention and stared straight ahead. 'I can only think that I forgot to lock the door, sir. I take full responsibility for that, and nobody else is to blame – *sir*!'

The General stood up and leaned forwards with his hands on the desk and Dory shrank back as he began to shake with rage.

'First you seem reluctant to take the Damaric Water – the sacred juice that keeps us alive – and now you admit to forgetting to lock the prisoner's cell. Black Guards do not forget things!' he shouted. 'Loss of memory is something humans – I repeat *humans* suffer from. Are you turning into a soft-headed human, Dalgo?'

Then he turned his attention to Dory. 'Not only are you a *liar*, but you are also a *spy*! And the punishment for spying is death.' There was a large sword hanging on the wall behind the General and he took it down and weighed it in his hands. 'Death,' he repeated, laying the sword carefully on his desk. 'Death!'

There was a murmur of approval from the assembled guards and one by one they took up the General's final word.

'Death!' they began to chant. 'Death, death, death, death...' until at last the General held up his hand for silence.

'And the honour of carrying out the punishment shall go to Captain Dalgo. Pick up the sword, Captain, and do your duty.'

***

A whole minute must have passed as Sir Tanty and the General faced each other in complete silence. Then a great gasp of disbelief arose from the crowd as the knight's visor rose and fell in a series of quick

168

movements, until finally revealing his eyes again which now blazed with a clear blue light.

'No,' he said, as he stepped towards Dory and placed his hand on his shoulder. 'No, I will not!'

The General raised his hand in the air in what must have been a prearranged signal and several guards grabbed Sir Tanty from behind and pulled him to the floor.

'Treachery!' screamed the General. 'A Loyal in black armour – another spy! I have had my doubts about you lately, Dalgo, if that is your real name. But a *Loyal Protector*, a dirty Loyal, and to think I promoted you myself!'

Once again, the guards raised their voices. 'Traitor, spy, dirty Loyal!' they cried, and then 'Fly, fly, fly,' over and over again.

The General held up his hand. 'Yes, fly,' he said, when the noise had died away. 'You shall fly from the top of this mountain before the day is over, or my name is not General Madza.'

He picked up the sword and approached Dory, who had now fallen to his knees.

'I will show you all how a Black Guard should behave,' he said, as Sir Tanty struggled to get free. He raised the weapon above his head and the guards jostled to get a better view. But something very strange was now happening to the General. Each time he tried to bring the weapon down, it stopped in mid-air and then rose again in jerky, mechanical movements. His head then began to move from side to side and up and down, and his knees buckled and then straightened, and soon his whole body was moving wildly as though he was a puppet under someone else's control. Within seconds, one of the guards began to act in the same peculiar way, and then another, and another, until, as though a contagious disease was spreading through their ranks, all the guards were dancing madly, flinging their arms in the air and bumping into one another, before falling to the floor in a heap of twitching bodies.

Dory looked up between his fingers as the General now began to sway from side to side and was just in time to scramble out of the way before he came crashing down beside him.

'Spy,' said the General, as their eyes met. The sword was still clasped in his hand and he made a final attempt to lift it. 'Little spy,' he said, in a voice now no more than a squeak. Then the sword rolled out of his grasp and he lay still.

Chapter 18

From other parts of the building, Dory could now hear the sounds of more guards collapsing, one after another, in a great echoing din, until at last there was nothing but silence, and he was suddenly aware of his own racing heartbeat.

His first thought was of Sir Tanty, and he found him lying beneath the bodies of two guards.

'Sir Tanty,' he whispered, 'can you move? Are you able to speak? It's me, Dory. But there was no reply and no sign of any movement from the knight, and when Dory tried to lift his visor, he found that it was clamped tightly shut.

The interior of the headquarters was now wrapped in a ghostly silence which added to the unreality of the scene facing Dory. As he moved slowly and carefully between the fallen Blaggards, he saw bodies that lay crouched over, as though suffering from stomach cramps, while many others appeared in the most impossible of poses: heads bent as if ready to fall off at any moment; legs stretched in opposite directions; arms raised as though appealing for help and feet and hands turned out at impossible angles.

At the top of the stairway, one guard lay curled up as though he was asleep, while another had somehow managed to stay on his feet, with his back against the wall, and as Dory edged past, the figure suddenly toppled over and bumped down the stone steps to end up sitting at the bottom. The powder had done its job, but was it permanent, he wondered?

Creeping past, and stepping over, the silent figures, after all that had just happened, was enough to make him believe that almost anything was possible. Once he was outside, he could hear sounds coming from one of the other entrances – the workers, perhaps, who were not yet aware that the guards had been destroyed and that they were now free.

The first entrance he looked into led to a large chamber containing a dozen or so horses. The second, he approached with more caution. Deep inside, he saw a huge cavern in which shadowy figures moved in and out of connecting rooms, and at the far end a team of humans was busy enlarging it to an even greater depth with picks and shovels. But, just as he was about to go inside to tell them the good news, he saw that not all of the Blaggards were done for. There was an angry shout and a guard carrying a crossbow came lumbering out of the shadows towards him.

'Stop!' he yelled, as Dory turned and ran, and he heard the wicked 'zing' of a bolt as it passed just over his head. Out in the open, he heard the guard gaining on him, but when he looked back he saw him stop and gaze in amazement at two Blaggards who were lying on the ground. But the guard didn't stop for long and, in his panic, Dory saw too late that he had run the wrong way, as in front of him now was the base of the mountain as it curved outwards. There was only one way to go and that was sideways and around it, but he was never going to make it in time.

The guard was now kneeling and taking aim, so in desperation Dory flung himself flat on the ground. There was a flash of red light, and when he looked up he saw the body of the guard fly through the air and then fall to the ground in a crumpled heap. And, to his delight and surprise, he saw Sir Mons striding towards it.

'Sir Mons!' cried Dory. 'Sir Mons, Is it really you!'

He looked down at the guard who lay quite still with smoke from the firepower strike pouring out of a hole in his breastplate.

'They're gone,' he said, 'they're gone. The Blaggards are finished. Where are Aimi and Sir Kitry? It was awful – Sir Tanty saved my life. He was so brave, and now he's gone as well.'

He lowered his head and tried hard to hold back the tears of sadness he felt for Sir Tanty, and of relief that his ordeal was over at last. Sir Mons took his hand and together they walked back to the headquarters where Sir Kitry, Tamlin and a joyous Aimi were waiting to greet him.

A head now cautiously peered out from the entrance of the workers' cavern, and then another, and soon a crowd of people – cooks, scientists, mechanics and labourers – came rushing out into the open, blinking and rubbing their eyes and shouting with joy.

'There is my father!' cried Aimi, as the last few prisoners ventured out. 'Father, over here!' She waved her arms in the air, before flinging them around his waist and hugging him close, as if she would never let him go.

Soon, the prisoners were asking questions: 'How did they get free?' 'Where were all the Blaggards?' To them, everything seemed to have changed so quickly. A guard lying on the ground with a hole in him? It didn't seem possible. Sir Mons went over to the main entrance and clanged his hands together until he had everyone's attention.

'This is a great day for Pellagaroo,' he cried. 'The Black Guards are no more!' A great cheer went up at this news, but the knight had more to say. He called Dory and Aimi to his side. 'These children, Dory and Aimi, are the ones mainly responsible for your freedom, but now they are tired and hungry. Please find some food for them if you can. In the meantime, Sir Kitry and I will tell you all that has happened, and discuss what we should do next.'

There was a kitchen of sorts at the back of the workers' cavern, where the children were provided with some of the plain and meagre rations from the Blaggards' stores, while Aimi and her father told each other of the things that had happened to them since leaving home. Both had a story to tell, but his tale – the account of soon being captured and made to work for the Blaggards – was as nothing compared to hers.

'Dear me' and 'Oh, my goodness', he kept saying, as Aimi told of how they had met the Bellman, of the imprisonment in the Rosegarden, and of their encounters with the Gargants – until he put up his hands and said 'Stop, stop! It is all too much to bear. To think that I have been the cause of all this. It is my curiosity, you see. I am very sorry, but life would be so very dull for me without it!'

***

There was great applause for the children when they went back outside. All the workers had now been given a brief account of their adventures and the cheering and clapping went on for such a long time that Sir Mons finally had to call for quiet.

'This appreciation is well deserved,' he said, 'but Dory and Aimi are two very tired children. Let them rest now while we continue to make plans for the future.'

But, tired as they were, neither Dory nor Aimi could relax, both being full of the memories of what had happened and excited at the prospect of going home.

'I must go and see Sir Tanty,' said Dory at last, 'and find out what's going to happen to him, what's left of him.'

Inside the headquarters, they saw the bodies of the Blaggards lying just where they had fallen. Several of the workers were wandering around, astonished at the sight of the mighty Blaggards who, in the end, had been conquered so easily. When they spotted the children they cheered loudly and thanked them again for their part in setting them free.

When Dory and Aimi reached General Madza's office, they found that Sir Mons and Sir Kitry were already there, along with the Professor. The knights had picked up Sir Tanty's body and now he lay on the General's desk with his arms folded, looking very peaceful and noble.

'Poor, brave Sir Tanty,' said Dory. 'He saved my life and then lost his own.'

'Well, not quite,' replied Sir Mons mysteriously. 'You tell them the good news, Kit.'

'We shall take him back to Castle Gardemal,' said Sir Kitry, 'where his system will be completely washed out until all the contaminated Damaric Water is gone. Then he will be rewired. His central memory should be all right. Oh, he may be a little forgetful at first, but with careful treatment he will soon be back to his old self.'

'We have come up with the idea of treating all the Blaggards as well,' added Sir Mons. 'These operations have been done before a couple of times on damaged Loyals, so there is no reason why they should not work on the Blaggards. Their minds will need certain readjustments. All the old memories and bad habits will be erased, and honour, compassion and loyalty instilled in their place. They will then make an excellent and proud addition to the Loyal Protectors. All that black paint will have to come off, though. Yes, there is much work ahead of us and the team at Gardemal.'

Sir Kitry laid his hand on Sir Tanty's chest and shook his head. 'One of the biggest tasks will be getting them back to the Castle Gardemal workshops. None of us is a lightweight. Just look at old Tanty here, and when I think how narrow and steep the mountain paths are in places...'

But now it was the Professor's turn to speak. 'No, no, Sir Knight.' He smiled broadly. 'You will not find that such a problem. At the rear of the stables is a broad passage that leads all the way back to Pellagaroo. It must have been a network of caves at one time, but the

Blaggards have had a team of workers enlarging it for years. One of them told me about it, and how some had tried to escape through it. They paid dearly for doing so.'

'So that is how they were able to arrive on their big horses!' exclaimed Sir Kitry. 'I often wondered about it. At one time, I thought they might have had a secret route, an easier way over the mountain. Well, the cunning old, er...'

Sir Mons laughed. 'Robots – I think the word can be used on this occasion!'

'Exactly so!'

But Dory was puzzled. 'You mean that all those horrible Blaggards can be changed into nice Loyals? Even General Madza?'

'*Even* General Madza,' Sir Kitry replied. 'Remember, Dory, it is the mind and not the body that makes us what we truly are.'

He looked at the General, who lay in a corner of the room like a broken doll, his head twisted around the wrong way and his arms and legs splayed out beneath him.

'Yes, even the bad General Madza can eventually become a good knight – but those silly feathers will have to go!'

***

It was decided that Sir Mons and the workers would stay behind in order to get the bodies ready for collection.

'Escort the children and the Professor back to the departure point, Kit,' he said. 'They must be longing to return home. I am going to send someone back to Gardemal. He can tell them what has happened and arrange for carts to be sent back through the tunnel to pick up the bodies.'

Dory looked up at the mountain, which towered above them. 'Just think, none of us needs to have climbed up there. We could've just ridden the horses right through the mountain!'

'Yes,' agreed Sir Kitry, 'and we would not have fallen into that horrible hole.'

Aimi shook her head. 'But then we would not have met Ranjee, who gave us the powder, and without that the Blaggards would still be around.' The knights nodded their agreement.

Now came the sad moment to say goodbye to Sir Mons.

'After all you have both been through,' he said solemnly, 'I do not suppose you will be in much of a hurry to visit Pellagaroo again. But if you did decide to in the future, I think you might find it to be a very different kind of place.'

'We have plans to rid ourselves of the Greymassers,' added Sir Kitry. 'Once the Blaggards have been converted, we shall have enough Loyals to form a constant guard around the Rosegarden. This will mean that no more victims will be able to be lured in for them to feed on and so they will gradually die out. The Rosegarden will then be destroyed and the land of

Pellagaroo will once again be without fear hanging over it.'

'And what will you do then,' asked Aimi, 'you and Sir Mons?'

Sir Kitry laughed. 'Well, I suppose I shall have to look after him, to stop him getting into trouble. There is a great area of what looks like uninhabited land on this side of the mountains. The Captain and I might ride across it one day to see what lies out there. Who knows, perhaps it goes on forever!'

Sir Mons nodded thoughtfully. 'Or comes out on the Other Side.'

Chapter 19

With a final wave, the children set off through the passage at the base of the mountain. They were riding Tamlin while Sir Kitry and the Professor sat astride a pair of horses from the stables. Here, too, the candlemoss grew in abundance, covering the damp walls and lighting the way through the sunless caves with a glow that was even brighter than that they had seen on the surface of the mountain.

Haloes of fuzzy light circled the dripping stalactites and these attracted huge, dark-winged moths which flew around them until they were dizzy, before falling to the floor and then flying back up again.

It was like entering another world, thought Dory, as they looked around in wonder. But soon they became aware of a strange sulphurous smell, which made breathing uncomfortable, and they were not sorry when, at last, they saw the exit shining in the far distance. They rode out, first through a small, dense wood and then on to the fields of Pellagaroo.

The sound of Jup's wild barking brought Florina to the front door as the children led the way up the garden path.

'Well!' she cried, when she had recovered from her astonishment. 'You are a pair and a half and no mistake! Where in the name of Pedro the pie pedlar have you been all this time?'

Sir Kitry quickly stepped forward. 'This is Aimi's father,' he said, turning to the Professor. 'They are all on their way home, but the children wanted to stop by to say goodbye and to apologise for running off as they did.'

But it was Florina's turn to say sorry after Sir Kitry had told her what had happened.

'Dear, brave children,' she said, after serving them up a good, hot meal, 'and to think how peeved I was after you left. Well, we all were. Poor Mother did cry so, and Father blamed himself – said he should've kept more of a watch over you.'

But when they had all gathered to say their sad farewells, Sir Kitry reminded everyone of the good that had come from the children's actions.

'If you *had* stopped them from following us, the Blaggards may never have been destroyed. In fact, I am beginning to think that, in some mysterious way, it was all meant to happen.'

***

A mixture of fear, sadness and happiness ran through Dory's mind as they approached the clifftop where they had first arrived. The last part of the journey had skirted the Great Thicket and Sir Kitry had also made certain that they would not pass within sight of the dreaded Rosegarden. Yet, despite the knight's presence, Dory still felt nervous. This, after all, was the spot where the grizlings had attacked them and not far away was the place where they had first encountered the Bellman. His sadness was caused by the thought of saying goodbye to Sir Kitry, who had proved to be such a loyal friend, but his heart was full of joy at the prospect of going home.

Dark clouds now came rearing up across the ocean on the back of a chill breeze, and for the first time since their arrival they saw the sky become overcast.

'The gloomy season will soon be with us,' said Sir Kitry. 'It does not last very long, just a few weeks usually, but when it comes we knights have to take extra care to get plenty of daylight. Sir Mons gets a bit grumpy,' he added with a chuckle, 'so it is best to keep out of his way for a while.'

It was time for them to leave, but no one made a move to do so, or to utter a single word of farewell. Even the horses seemed to catch the sad mood, hanging their heads low and shifting restlessly from foot to foot.

'Off you go then,' said Sir Kitry at last, 'and bring some sunshine with you on your next visit. Hurry along now, before the impossible happens. Loyal Protectors are not programmed to cry and I do not want to be the first one to achieve it!'

Dory went first.

'Make sure you move to the back of the tower when you arrive,' the Professor had said. 'We do not want to bump into you when it is our turn.'

The return journey was almost exactly the same as the outward one, except at the very last moment, when, instead of smoothly touching down, the landing place seemed to rise up to meet him. Then his feet made gentle contact with the tower step and he was inside. A sad-looking Aimi followed, but before he could ask her what was wrong the Professor, too, came rushing in.

'Well done, well done!' he said, hugging Aimi and giving Dory a pat on the back. He looked out of the tower window and surveyed the scene below, as though to make sure that everything was still there.

'There were times when I thought I would never see my home again,' he said, 'nor my darling daughter. Her mother named her well. "Aimi" means "loving" and without her love I suppose I would still be in the hands of the Blaggards.'

He walked around the tiny room, rubbing his hands together and talking rapidly. Suddenly, he seemed almost like a different man. 'So much to do,' he went on, 'so much work to catch up with. Now let me see, what is for the best? Yes, yes, that is it, we must go down. So much to do.'

He pressed a button on the wall and the capsule door slid open. 'You first, Dory,' he said. 'No room for three of us in there.'

Once Dory was inside, the Professor stretched in, made an adjustment to the hands on one of the dials, flicked a switch and then closed the door. But Dory was in for a shock. Instead of the swift, smooth ride he had experienced before, the machine stopped halfway down the tower. Something's wrong, he thought, the capsule's stopped and I'm trapped inside! Panic gripped him as he looked around at the confining walls.

'Help!' he shouted. 'Help! Let me out!'

And then the capsule moved up a little and stopped, and then moved a little more. So it went on in a series of stops and starts until, at last, he heard a sharp 'click', as though a cog had been engaged. With a quiet hum, the machine began to spin. Around and around it went, slowly at first, then gradually gathering speed until the walls around him became a blur and he was unable to move, pinned as he was to the walls by the outward force. Just as he thought he was about to faint, the spinning came to an abrupt stop. The capsule seemed to dissolve around him and he was propelled out into open space, weightless and afloat in a cloud of mist.

Now came light, and he saw the sun move in an arc above his head, then quickly fall beneath the rim of the earth. Then the moon followed, trailing a stream of stars that scattered across the sky before falling into their correct positions. This cycle of nights and days continued until, at last, the sun remained and he began to fall. Down and down he went, turning slow cartwheels in the air in a most pleasurable way. He began to wonder if he had died and thought that, if he had, he didn't mind at all because he felt so much at peace. Things had happened recently – bad things, it seemed – but whatever they were, they hadn't happened to him, had they? They must have happened to another Dory, a more adventurous boy, while all he wanted to do was to continue falling effortlessly through the sky. And then the earth came rushing up to meet him and thumped him heavily in the back, and he closed his eyes and was very still.

***

How long he lay there he couldn't tell, but as he slowly regained his senses the sweet, earthy scent of the grass that curled between his fingers told him exactly where he was. He saw, even before he opened his eyes, a single cloud in the sky above his head and knew that he was surrounded by a vast moorland that stretched away to the far-off sea.

My kite, he thought, as he sat up and opened his eyes. My kite will have flown away. But, when he looked around, he saw that it was lying on the ground just a few feet away. He picked up the kite. Everything looked so normal. It was almost as though he had never been away. Been away? Yes, he was certain that he had been away somewhere, but where?

High in the sky above his head, a hawk was drifting on the warm currents of air that rose from the moorland. It was something he had seen many times before, but now he saw the bird grow large and black, making him instinctively crouch in fear, until he saw it return to its normal size. Now, as he began to run home, strange images as if from a nightmare began to appear – a little girl smiled at him from out of the bushes; a clump of trees, stunted and misshapen by the winds, became two knights on horseback and the solitary cloud now turned into a soft, grey mass that grew larger and began to descend over him.

On and on he ran, still clutching his kite, until a great house with tall crooked chimneys and a dark tower rushed at him and scooped him up in its shadows.

***

'A mild concussion,' said the doctor as he prepared to leave. 'He must have had a fall and knocked his head. Keep him in bed for a few days. Peace and quiet is all he needs. I'll pop in again soon to see how he's getting on.'

Dory had been found and brought home by some neighbours who had been picnicking.

'He was talking such nonsense,' his mother said. 'Seemed to think he'd been away for days and missed his birthday tea, but he's only been gone a few hours. Here's his cake ready on the table. He said his kite had lost some of its tail, but it's done no such thing.'

Dory slept, dreamless and unafraid in the room with its striped curtains, ticking clock and bedside table, which was all just as it should have been when at last he opened his eyes. It was night, but the room was clearly lit by the light of the moon. He was home. He had taken a tumble while flying his kite. He had been knocked out and had had some strange dreams that he couldn't remember. It was all quite simple and now he was home where he belonged.

He looked up at the ceiling and, despite his aching tiredness, a story began to unfold before his eyes, a new story that seemed to be ready to write itself. There would be a little girl in it and her name would be...? Well, that didn't matter for now. He'd think of one later. She would live with her father, an inventor, and one day he would disappear and she would go in search of him. There would also be a boy who would go with her and they would have lots of adventures, some good and some not so good, in a strange land. There would be knights in armour – you'd have to have those – and one of them would be brave and kind, a bit like Sir Lancelot, but he could also be funny, and sometimes sad, and he would always be a true and loyal friend, a kind of protector.

There was a thin crack in the ceiling in the shape of a large letter 'U' and above it was a line of dark lumps in the plaster where the damp had once got in. This was obviously a map of the country where the adventures would take place. The 'U' was the outline of the land, which jutted out into a mysterious ocean, and the lumps in the plaster were a mountain range that marked its northern boundary. The rest of the ceiling was flat and colourless, so everything there would be unknown territory.

He sat up and reached for his notebook and pen, but the effort proved to be too much for him and they slipped from his grasp. An owl called out from a tree in the garden, a cloud passed across the face of the moon and the room was dark once more.

'To be continued,' he muttered, as his head fell back on the pillow. He closed his eyes, and soon he was once again up on the lonely moors, following a wayward kite and running, running, running...

The end